MARK HEMS

SIGN OF THE TIME

A NOVEL

ISBN-13: 978-1482046090

- Acknowledgments -

Special thanks to Hayley and my family for your unwavering support in all that I do – I love you all very much!

And many thanks to all of the people who gave me invaluable feedback during the writing of this novel. Thanks to Mom, Julie, and my good friends Adam Robson and Stephen Bashow.

This book is based on actual events.

- The Abyss -

Into the darkness I fell as my soul was stripped apart.

I was being *erased.* Piece by piece, memory by memory, thought by thought - the very fabric of my being unravelling into the night like the threads of an elaborate tapestry. I struggled to hold on to life as the cold wind ravaged my mind.

But it was not yet the end.

Just as I thought I was doomed to live out eternity in darkness, lightning lit up the void with a *bang* and I hurtled towards its source. I tried to shield my eyes against the glare but realized I couldn't. My hands didn't seem to be there anymore – my *body* didn't seem to be there anymore! Terrified, I was helpless as I fell into the lightning. And witnessed my own birth: Screaming, I emerged from my mother's womb, dripping with blood and warmth and life.

The world was radiant with colour and verve and the sound of my own crying threatened to deafen me – but I was alive! There was an odd feeling of weightlessness as I was carried through the air and then my mother's face came into view: tears streaming down red cheeks as she took me into her arms. She hugged me close and my heart leapt with the sheer wonder of the moment. I wanted to talk to her - to explain what had happened, but as I opened my mouth to speak the lightning sounded with a bang and I was ripped forwards in time.

I found myself padding on almost new feet to a young man I barely recognized as my father before the lightning ripped me away again.

Bang!

I saw my first day at school, spraying macaroni with gold paint.

Bang!

My big sister placing a plaster on my knee.

Bang!

Tiny happy faces crammed with cake and joy at a forgotten birthday party.

Bang!

My long dead dog, Benjy.

Bang!

My first kiss – a flurry of pig-tales and red ribbons.

Bang!

My brother being born, his little red face crusty with snot.

Bang! Bang! Bang!

The memories came faster and faster - all of the people I had known, all of my triumphs, all of my failures. Until I sensed with terror that the final event was approaching. With a churning dread I heard the screeching of tyres, felt the cold wind in my face and saw the anguished faces of a friend and an enemy spinning around me before a relentless ocean rushed up to envelop us.

And then nothing.

I was once again plummeting through the darkness. I tried to remember how I got there but with growing dismay I realized that my memories had been eaten up by the darkness, discarded in time. But still I fell, nothing more than a collection of thoughts now - only just able to recognize that the farther I fell, the less I became. *Soon I will be nothing,* I thought, and with this notion, a barely conscious fragment of self questioned the nature of its state and had an epiphany: if there were a *correlation* between my descent and my demise, then what if I could somehow reverse the trend, if I could fight gravity's pull and *ascend*? What if death was simply a type of downward current, reflected by my descent? Could I reverse the current? Could I somehow climb back to life? And what if I pushed farther, beyond even the ceiling of life, perhaps to its final conclusion? Where might that lead?

What if the single, most important purpose of all life was to evolve will to the extent that it might defy the mortal coil, break the physical bonds and hurtle skywards in an attempt to better itself. To better the Universe?

But it was too late.

It seemed my fate was not to become nothing but to return to *every*thing. I assimilated this knowledge as a drop in a fountain returning to its source: I was now part of something much greater - part of everything, pure and eternal. But with this ultimate experience of oneness came an immense feeling of loss for the fragment of self that I had been and a tiny filament of that self rebelled against the ubiquitous force that held it. I knew for certain now that the person I had been would be lost forever, absorbed in the very fabric of existence - unless I attempted to break free. So, barely functioning as an autonomous mind, I struggled to recall the epiphany I had experienced about the nature of the currents of life and death and found that in this pure state, with no physical limitations to bind me, merely thinking about life pushed me upwards a fraction. Holding on to that thought I began to rise, *willing* myself upwards. And very slowly the strands of self that had been unwound began to wrap themselves back around me - my mind a spool for the experiences that had shaped me. But as I continued to move upwards, faster and faster - like a snowball gathering substance and momentum, I also reacquired my earthly faculties of reason and doubt. With these faculties also came fear, and, realizing my precarious state halfway between everything and *some*thing, I momentarily panicked and lost control, plummeting back towards oblivion.

My entire being *screamed* and, just as the all consuming everything rushed up to envelop me, I closed my mind and focussed on that one pure shard of will, of *hope.*

And my descent reversed. For what seemed like an age I ascended a featureless void: like scaling a mountain in a blizzard. But as I ascended higher and higher, tiny details began to emerge. To start with there was only the barest suggestion of things; the rough, jagged surface of a rock, the white fluff of a cloud. But the more I concentrated on these features, the more they began to acquire clarity, and the higher I ascended, the more vivid and extraordinary they became: looking down into the abyss I now saw legions of cities, each piled on top of the next, spiralling down to infinity.

I found myself running along rooftops following that spiral ever upwards. And as I ascended, my speed accelerated until the cities became galaxies and the galaxies became mere strands of something greater; everything connected in a spiralling spider's web. Eventually I found myself vaulting over vast interstellar canyons, swimming through the annals of time, sprinting through the colour frequencies: Forever pushing up, *up*.

It was then that the second epiphany struck me: the life current was not mutually tied to the idea of *up* but seemed to be a product of idea *itself*. Indeed, I felt that the more intricate, the more creative my imaginings were, the more swiftly I ascended and the more powerful my creative imagination became.

Until a sharp whisper threatened to shatter the fragile reality I had constructed. 'Hems!'

My upwards motion ceased abruptly. That name was familiar. It was *my* name. Was this voice merely a product of my imagination? Whatever it was, I couldn't allow it to threaten my ascent – if I fell back into the abyss...

A deafening crackling crumbled the walls of self that I had reconstructed and, panicked, I began to fall.

Hold on! HOLD ON!

'Huuuuuuup, Hems, quick. Oy!' A nudge to the shoulder shattered my concentration and I plummeted - into the world.

Intense, vibrant colour flooded my senses and I found myself sitting on a bed in a gloomy room. A haze of smoke dancing in front of my eyes, emanating from a gleaming bronze pipe. The smoke threatened to entrance me and I suddenly felt nauseous.

What the hell just happened? I thought, my memories returning in an instant. I had been smoking pot with my friend Terry who had taken great pleasure in trying to get me as wasted as possible, presumably to test the limits of my currently extremely fragile psyche. And test them he had – the experience had clearly nearly broken me.

I received another sharp prod to the shoulder and looked up to see Terry's face looming over me. His smile was menacing - the grimace of Death's best salesman. He gestured for me to take the pipe with a mixture of glee and hunger in his eyes.

'Mno' I managed to blurt, my voice barely audible over the wailing of guitars issuing from the sound system.

He forced the pipe into my hands, the cheer in his eyes replaced with malice as he stoked the burning bounty in the bowl of the pipe. I knew that to resist would be futile, particularly in my current, precarious state. I took the hot pipe in quivering hands, fearful that it would burn my fingers, and looked up at Terry. Still holding his last lungful of smoke, he pushed a searing lighter into my free hand and urged me to plunge back into the darkness.

I made one last pitiful attempt to refuse and received a sharp poke to the ribs and a look of murderous intent. I knew that another pipe would render me even more helpless, but I simply did not possess the courage to overcome him. And so, in an irrational move to hold on to my last vestige of dignity, I presented a show of strength. Bringing the pipe to my lips, I lit the bowl and deeply inhaled white hot smoke into blistered lungs. I was only too aware of greedy eyes intently focussed on their prey, to ensure that I would be truly destroyed. Breathing in until my lungs were set to burst, the smouldering *black* began to turn to white.

'Hold it in Hems! Come on horse lungs!'

Against all instinct, as if obeying the suggestions of a hypnotist, I held my breath as he began the countdown.

And so I fell into the darkness once more. By now I was all too familiar with this (metaphor?), but I was also very close to evacuating my dinner all over the carpet and I didn't think that I could suffer another indignity. And so I attempted to weather the storm, unable to open my eyes; prey to the onslaught of dark imagery that lurked within the depths of my sub conscious.

I didn't want to get into this state, in fact I never intended to smoke the pot in the first place – particularly not in such vast quantities. But somehow Terry always managed to talk me into it. And as soon as I had endured a bong or two my defences were obliterated and I was easy prey. I know that sounds strange, *prey*, but that's exactly how I felt, because you see, Terry was a predator. On the surface he seemed clean cut - smartly dressed, eloquently spoken, intelligent and good natured. In fact he was the sort of person you might expect to see running for Mayor, such was his ability to charm. But this exterior was nothing but a sham belied by the coldness in his eyes.

I was faintly aware of the doorbell ringing as if the sound had travelled to me as I sank beneath the sea. I heard muffled voices and became suddenly quite panicked.

It was Bob and Jed.

Jesus! I couldn't cope with more people – I was finding it hard enough to keep it together with the one person I had in the room already!

'Hey, what's this! What are you two doing here!' asked Terry.

'Jed's been kicked out.'

'Ooooh!' Terry clapped his hands and whooped, clearly relishing this bit of news. 'What happened – Spikey Mikey have another fit or did Eileen find out you've been stealing from her again? No way, she did didn't she! Ooh! Ooh!'

'Shut up, Terry,' uttered Jed.

I had managed to emerge from my pit, open my eyes and lift up my head to observe all of this as Bob sat down next to me on the bed.

'Alright Hemsy.'

'Alright' I said in a croaky, barely audible voice.

'Hems look's fucked man. Look at your eyes mate. Fuck. Total red eye! Ha hA!' For some reason when Bob laughed he liked to place extra emphasis on the last 'a'.

Terry came over and looked me over. For some reason he pulled an exaggerated mean face.

'Hems!' he growled, giving me a sharp poke to the stomach.

Terry turned back to Jed who had started crumbling hash into his pipe.

'What's this! Here two minutes and already he's firing up! Nice one! What have you got?'

'Just soap bar.'

'Let's have a look.'

Jed passed the hash over to Terry to assess.

'Not bad. Red seal?'

'Dunno, maybe.'

'It is, I had the same stuff the other day – got it from Fudge.'

'Nice.'

'Have you got any of that black left?'

'Not much – Hemsy's caned it all!'

They turned to look at me as I slowly raised my head and they all burst out laughing.

'Right come on then horse lungs' said Terry looking at me and gesturing towards Jed's pipe.

'Nah man – I need this right now' said Jed, looking about twenty years older and wiser than he actually was and narrowly saving me from a heart attack.

'Oooh! But fuckin Hemsy's been practicing man! I want to show you his horse lungs!'

Jesus no. Not now. The last five were bad enough!

To my relief, Jed simply started toking on his pipe before blowing smoke in Terry's face and smiling slyly.

'Where are you going to sleep?' I heard someone say and then realised it was me.

'Dunno, was thinking about going into town to see Fudge, get fucked off my tits and sleep on the beach.'

'Shit,' I said, 'Have you got enough money?'

Jed laughed. 'Just twenty, I had fifty but I put thirty into the fruit machine.'

'Where did you get fifty quid from?' asked Terry.

Jed just gave him a mischievous look.

'Bumped-ah!' exclaimed Bob. 'He's been at the leccy metre again hasn't he!'

'Nooo! Ha ha. You sly dog Jed! Is that why she kicked you out – for stealing money from the electric metre?'

'No, she kicked me out for stealing money from the gas metre!'

- Old Honker -

It had been a couple of months since my experience of the abyss and in that time, Terry had developed a hearty appetite for Sherry (or any other cheap alcohol he could get his hands on). At the moment he was desperately trying to convince me to be an accomplice to his daily book thieving crimes. When you're on the dole, £37.50 a week minus a £7 rent contribution really doesn't go very far, especially when you're financing drink and drug habits.

'No way man, we can't keep doing this!' I said, adamant that I would not give way this time.

'Ok, just listen, if you don't want to do it that's fine. You've helped me out and I appreciate that Hems...'

'Ok...' I was almost fooled.

'But, I just worry that if you're not there watching my back that I'll get caught...I need some Hemsy magic on my side man! I don't know how you manage to distract them but it works...'

'For fuck sake man we've been doing this every day for weeks, we can't get away with this forever – we are *going* to get caught!'

'Look, this will be the last time, Mark, I swear!'

I hesitated before saying once again, 'Terry I'm sorry but I'm not doing this again – I told you yesterday.'

A sudden change of tact and Terry's face changed from the earnest face of a faithful friend to that of a disgraced father.

'*FINE!* Hems if you want to do that, if you think so little of me after all these years that I've looked out for you man!'

'Oh, bollocks!'

'No, it's alright, I'm going. Fuck it, I need a drink man. I haven't got time for this, I'm going to do over Smiths...'

'Oh for fuck's sake, you do that and you're definitely going to get caught and this time there'll be no slap on the wrist!'

Terry suddenly turned back to face me. 'Exactly! I probably *will* get caught 'cause I won't have you watching my back! But clearly you're fine with that so I'll just go.'

He started to walk for the door.

I should have let him go - this routine was almost a daily occurrence and the manipulation transparent, yet somehow he always knew how to press my buttons.

'Alright!' I said, exasperated. Though Terry had his back toward me I could sense a sly smile and an almost tangible rubbing of his hands. When he turned around to face me, his entire persona had magically transformed from pleading victim to chat show host as he launched into his plan.

'Ok, this time it has to be good. Like I say I do intend this to be the last time, but for that it's got to be bigger and therefore a bit riskier.'

'Oh, come on man, why do we have to do this!?'

'You know why, I've got no fucking food man – how am I supposed to eat? Have you seen how fucking skinny I'm getting?'

'Yeah, like that's the reason.'

'Are you calling me a liar, Hems? Look...' Flustered and turning very red, Terry fished out a worn Quicksilver wallet from his back pocket and aggressively forced it into my hands.

'That's all I've got in the whole fucking world man. Check it, how much is in there?'

'I don't know.'

'Fucking look!'

I looked for notes and found none so unzipped the change pocket and found a twenty pence piece and two pennies.

'Twenty two pence.'

Saying nothing he yanked the wallet back out of my hands. Looking at me as if I had insulted him on a deep level, he assumed the guise of a dying man appealing to me for an ounce of goodness.

'If you want the truth, Hems I haven't eaten in days...'

'But I cooked that black bean thing yesterday...'

There was a moment's hesitation. 'Well yeah but I threw that up...'

'Well that's what happens when you drink two and half bottles of White Lightning!'

'No, that's what happens when *you* feed me shit! Seriously though, I'm not well at the moment man, I've got some flu thing – you know that. Look we haven't got time for this, I promise, when we do this we can go to old Honker's, get our cash and go straight for a nice slap up breakfast. Doesn't that sound good to you, Hemsy?'

I took a deep breath.

'If you can promise me a hundred percent that this will be the last time... we'll get some food and *no* more drink. You've got to promise me man!'

'Definitely Hemsy. Hundred percent man.' He agreed, crossing his heart as if butter wouldn't melt.

Ten minutes later and I was at the counter of W.H Smiths. Upstairs where it was quiet. It was a dreary Tuesday morning in October and customers were thin on the ground.

Perfect conditions for Terry's plan.

The man at the counter looked like he had been there for a very long time, the colour sapped from his face to match the grey of the day.

'Can I help you?' He mustered, beady eyes perched over wire-framed spectacles.

'I hope so, I'm trying to find a book by a German Philosopher, I believe his name is Friederick Nietzsche.'

'Ok...' he replied and turned around to face a dated database terminal that painted his face with a green glow. There we go, now there was at least a bit of colour.

I risked a quick glance to the doorway in time to see Terry surreptitiously entering the room, all dressed in black like a cat burglar or the milk tray man. He was heading for his special blind spot, right beneath one of the security cameras that was angled *slightly* too high.

'Sorry, what was the name again?' ventured the clerk.

My head shot back to the counter.

'Friederick Nietzsche.'

'How do you spell that?'

'Erm, F...R...E...no sorry, F, R, I... '

'Yep.'

'...E, D, E, R, I, C, K'

'Yyyyep.'

'And the surname I think is spelt, N, E, no...N...I, E, T, S, Z... no hold on I think the Z might be before the S. Sorry, let's try that again.'

The store clerk sighed as he erased the letters he had just typed, but gave me a look of good humour. I didn't think I'd be able to mess him around for too long though so I hoped that Terry was nearly finished.

'Right, I think it's N, I, E... T, er Z, S... C, H, E...yeah that sounds about right.

'Ok, let's try that...' The clerk said, typing the letters into his terminal.

There was a pause of a few moments whilst the terminal whirred through its data and then a number of entries appeared on the screen. ‘Here we go, ok was there a specific book you were after?’

‘Do you have *Thus Spake Zarathustra*?’

‘Let’s see...’ there was a pause as the man searched through the listings. ‘Ah, here it is - we do stock it but it looks like it’s currently out of stock I’m afraid. I could order it in for you if you like?’

At that moment, Terry marched past us with his backpack bulging.

I don’t know why he couldn’t just walk like a normal person in a shop, like someone who *might* actually be looking to buy something. No, he had to march about like a bloody storm trooper with his chest stuck out and his head down. Basically, the most noticeable person in the world and the *first* person you would suspect of being a shop lifter.

Momentarily distracted I looked back at the clerk, who fortunately *somehow* hadn’t noticed Terry’s departure and was more interested in getting my response.

‘Erm, sorry was in a world of my own there for a minute – what did you say?’

'I said we don't have the book in stock. Would you like to order it in?'

'Oh, no that's ok thanks, I was hoping I could get something today. But thanks for looking for me anyway.'

The clerk gave me a humourless smile and tapped a few more keys before presumably returning to whatever he had been doing before I had interrupted his hum drum existence with my intriguing difficult-to-spell-surname search.

In order to avoid arousing suspicion by leaving immediately, I walked over to one of the book stands and started paging through a random book before realizing I was in the romance section and becoming mildly embarrassed. Mr Grey looked at me with one eyebrow ever so slightly raised and I hastily returned the steamy novel to its shelf and made my way to the exit. Yeah, no one was going to suspect me of shoplifting. Being a big girl's blouse, maybe.

Outside, the wind was whipping up off the beach and a cold breeze laden with salt water assaulted me. I received an equally warm reception from Terry who grabbed me by the arm and gave me a look filled with daggers.

'Where the fuck have you been, Hems!?'

'What? Well I'm not going to come marching right after you so that we look like a *team* of shop lifting storm troopers am I?'

'Shut up Hems! Just hurry up.'

'Terry slow down man, you just look dodgy walking about like that.'

'Just fucking hurry up!'

We walked briskly through the town centre and I shivered with the mixture of adrenaline, fear and excitement that was flowing through me. Rounding a corner our destination came into view: a small second hand bookshop with a picture of a globe on its worn sign. I think it used to be called 'World Books' but the print had long since perished. We escaped the rain before it had a chance to really get going and walked into an oasis of warmth, incense and dust. It was the sort of place you might expect to purchase a gremlin from a wise old man. As we entered, a bell chimed to signal our presence.

Old Honker as Terry had referred to her was sitting behind a low counter studying a large book, which seemed to be about insects and algae, judging by the illustrations.

'Good day,' said Terry instantly transforming into a good natured and polite gentleman, apparently from the thirties. Psychopaths never seemed to understand how to talk to people.

‘Hello,’ she responded, looking up and reminding me why Terry had nicknamed her so cruelly. She did indeed possess an *enormous* nose, but behind that, nestled beneath a school teacher’s half-moon glasses, were dark eyes that shone with intelligence.

‘I was saving the best of my books for last...’ Terry said, removing his bag; his muscular and slightly aggressive movements belying his supposedly good nature. Putting the bag heavily onto the table he opened it up to reveal a treasure trove. Over the last few weeks (how had we gotten away with it for that long?) he had developed a technique of swiping half a shelf of books straight into his open bag.

Having had some experience of Terry’s technique over the last few weeks, and recognizing the desperation in his eyes, Honker played it cool. She knew very well that this was brand new stolen merchandise - hard backs each worth between ten and thirty pounds.

‘Well I’m a bit short this week,’ she began, ‘I don’t know if I can afford to buy any more of...your books.’

‘Really? But these are great books! Look at this one this cost...’ he checked the price on the back ‘thirty pounds! I’m sure you’d get a good price for this.’

'Hmmm these sorts of books haven't been selling very well lately...'

'And look at this one!' Terry continued, picking out a book on Astrology. 'This one would go really well in your magic section over there. Great book, my Gran bought it for Christmas last year. I'm only getting rid of it because I'm a bit hard up, you know, these are hard times.'

'Yes, they are indeed. Ok, the best I can do is fifty pence a book, but I only want these.' She pushed several books to one side.

Unperturbed, Terry continued his barter. 'Well, let's discuss the price in a *moment*, first of all I really want to show you this, now this *is* special.'

When he was sure he had gotten the best price that he could we left the shop and started making our way back through the town on auto pilot.

'Fucking big nosed bitch!' growled Terry out of nowhere.

I looked at him questioningly.

'There had to be about fifteen books there.'

'How many did she take in the end?'

'About fucking twelve.'

'Shit. How much did she give you, eight was it?'

'Seven fifty.'

'Shit. Well it doesn't matter, at least you got something and you can get some food now.'

'Yeah. Just want to pop in here for a minute.' He said taking a sharp right into the off license before I had a chance to argue.

'Come on man, you said you were just going to get food.' I pleaded.

'Shut up, Hems. Bottle of fortified cream sherry please.'

The shop assistant, a girl who didn't look old enough to be selling alcohol, turned around and surveyed the liquor shelf. Terry helped her by indicating the one with the red label.

Returning to the counter, the girl handed over the bottle and keyed the price into the till.

'Two twenty two please.'

Terry fished out his recently replenished wallet and handed over some of the change he had received from Old Honker.

'Thanks.' Terry said before barging past me towards the exit.

Back on the street the rain had stopped and Terry wasn't going to waste a moment to open his prize - after all his hard work.

'Wanna see a neat party trick, Hems?'

It must have been a rhetorical question because before I could answer he had put the bottle to his lips, tipped back his head and proceeded to swallow the thick liquid down in long gulps. I presumed that he was just going to have a few swigs but he had perfected the ability to simply open his gullet and let the alcohol flow straight down his throat.

It took less than ten seconds to finish the entire bottle, the sherry disappearing as if by magic.

Tipping his head forward and taking the bottle from his lips Terry was instantly drunk and narrowly avoided falling sideways into oncoming traffic.

'Whoa there! Are you alright Terry – fuck, can't believe you did in the whole bottle!'

'Skillz' he burped loudly 'that pay the billz!'

'Ahuh.'

He started walking towards me and stumbled right and then left before finding his balance.

It was going to be a long day.

- Wingnut -

We made our way back to Terry's bedsit at the back of the bus station where he shared a house with an assortment of alcoholics and junkies, including an old man whom he had nicknamed *Wingnut* on account of his big ears. Every time I had ever seen the old man he was so drunk that he couldn't string two words together.

Opening the front door, Terry walked through and knocked loudly on Wingnut's bedroom door.

'Oi Wingnut, got a visitor for ya.' Terry said, stumbling against the door and burping loudly.

I put my hands up to Terry questioning why he was disturbing the old man and heard a rumbling in the room beyond the door and a thud as the man presumably walked into the wall.

Terry pounded on the door. 'Oi Wingnut! Open the door, it's important.'

I heard a scrabbling and then the old man was standing before us, one eye black and closed, the other half closed. A stench of whiskey and urine wafted into the hallway to mix with the smell of damp carpet.

'Yerrrrr?' said Wingnut, his head bobbing from side to side as if the bones in his neck had been removed.

'Look who I've bought to see you! You remember Mark...' he paused, 'the *policeman*.'

Wingnut looked alarmed and staggered back into the room, looking at me questioningly, eyes now wide.

'Don't listen to him man, I'm not the police, he's just a twat.' I said.

I turned round to look at Terry who was nodding his head at the old man and mouthing *PO-LEESS*

'Don't be a dick man.' I said to Terry and he let out a rip roaring laugh. I turned back to the old man, who was now half lying on the bed, still watching me with a look of uncertainty on his face. Surveying the room it was no wonder he had fallen over, the floor was littered with bits and pieces of random junk and in the corner stood a large oxygen tank, which he had apparently bought to go diving, though I doubted he'd ever manage to use it.

'Don't worry mate, everything's fine, ok? What did you do to your head?' I said.

'Flllluuurr gof!'

'Playing golf?' I ventured.

He hiccupped, closed his eyes for a moment, refocused and then said:

'Pa pa polise fark...<hic>...fah fak arf...'

'Fark arf? Oh, fuck off! Ok, well same to you too mate.' I closed the door quietly behind me.

Terry was still laughing his head off. 'He really likes you Hems.'

'Twat.' I said and followed him up the stairs to his bedsit. The house was in a bad state of disrepair and I worried that the stairs would give way against our weight.

Reaching his bedsit, Terry barged at the door with his shoulder. It never opened properly so he had to give it a kick, dislodging saw dust from the rotten door panel to join a small pile of wood splinters on the stained carpet. Entering the room I was affronted with a strange smell of chicken and disinfectant. Terry ambled over to his stereo and, putting down his keys he fished out a CD and placed it into the drive. After a moment the speakers crackled and the opening track to Dr Dre's, *The Chronic* began to play.

Moving his arms in supposedly gangster like gestures, Terry mouthed along with the rapper: 'This is dedicated to the niggers that was down from day one [CLUNK

CLUNK] welcome to death row. Like we always do about this time!'

I sat down on the bed and lit a cigarette as Terry retrieved his pipe from the side of the stereo.

'How did he get those bruises on his face?' I asked.

'Who?' Terry said.

'Wingnut. He had a black eye and a big gash on his head.'

'Oh him, he's always getting into scrapes, he gets so fucked he bangs into things, he's got a new bruise every day.'

'Poor bastard.' I said.

Terry just laughed and started loading his pipe. 'Jed threatened to shoot him last night.'

'What? Why?' I said, alarmed.

'He wouldn't share his whiskey! Cheap bastard.'

'That guy freaks me out.'

'Jed?'

'Yeah, I mean all this shit about shooting people, do you reckon he's really got a gun up there?'

'Shhh shh shh! Didn't I tell you, Hems?' Terry said whispering and turning the stereo up so that I had to draw close to hear what he was saying. 'the other day I woke up to a gunshot and nearly shit myself. He was shooting at birds on the roof!'

I raised my eyebrows.

'Seriously, Hems, I wouldn't fuck with that bloke, he's got some issues. Scary fucking eyes too...'

'Yeah,' I said, 'He's not right.'

'Evil.' He said nodding. 'Did I tell you about this book I've been reading? 'The World's most evil men'?'

'Yeah, you were telling me about Hitler and stuff last week.'

Terry seemed to be obsessed by serial killers and mass murderers.

'Have you heard of, Francois Duvalier, AKA Papa Doc, Hems?'

'No,' I said shaking my head, 'who's that when he's at home?'

'Fuck Hems! Do you know how many people this guy killed?' said Terry, narrowing his eyes.

I shrugged.

'Only an estimated thirty fucking thousand! Can you even begin to contemplate the enormity of that figure, Hems?'

'Not really, that *is* quite a lot of killing. He must have been a busy man, I mean, that's a *full* schedule!'

Terry ignored me and continued.

'And you never even hear about it!'

'Well I'm hearing a lot about it...'

'He modelled himself on this voodoo god of the dead, *Baron Samedi*. Ever hear about him, Hems?'

'Oh, yes I know all about *Baron Samedi*.'

'Really?' said Terry, surprised.

'No.'

'Don't be a prick Hems, I'm trying to teach you here!'

'Alright, chill out man, I'm just messing about.'

Terry was still quite drunk and his face was flushed red.

'I mean Jesus man! How *fucking* fucked up! Thirty thousand!'

'Yeah...'

'You know what he used to do?' He said, coming a little too close to my face and peering down at me with fierce eyes. 'He'd send out his voodoo troops, Tont...Tont*on*...' he shouted '...Macates and they would come and fucking *slice* you up Hems.' He mimed the act, slicing his fingers up my ribs painfully.

'Alright, chill out man!' I said, backing away onto the bed.

Terry sat back down, his eyes full of anger as if he was attempting to personify the evil of which he spoke. Remembering his pipe, he sat up, lit the bowl and inhaled until his lungs were almost full, and then sucked up twice more. Holding his breath he gestured for me to take the pipe and I refused.

'No thanks mate, I'm smoking this.' I said holding up my cigarette.

Terry looked at me with anger in his eyes and said, 'Evil weed! You ought to quit that shit, Hems, that shit will kill you.'

I almost laughed and wanted to call him a hypocrite but decided to let it lie. Instead I decided it was time to leave. 'Anyway mate, I'm gonna leave you to it, gotta go and do some washing and sort my stuff out for work tomorrow.'

'Fairish nuff' he said, holding out his hand for me to shake. I bent down to shake it and he crushed down on my fingers, looking for signs of weakness in my eyes. Instinctively, I grabbed his wrist and twisted.

'Fucking hell Hems! Just giving you a friendly hand shake!'

'Yeah right.'

'Oi, oi, hold on hold on, before you go I've got a present for you.' He bent over and picked up the bag he used to rob the shop. Opening it, he pulled out the remaining stolen merchandise: a book on palmistry, an SAS survival guide and a special pack of Tarot cards that came with an accompanying book.

'Take your pick.' He said.

'That's alright thanks.'

'Come on Hems, you earned this.'

Looking at the selection I *was* tempted by the Tarot pack and, seeing my interest, Terry picked it up and thrust it into my hands.

'Come on Hems, take it.'

'*Ok*, thanks.'

'Oh *go* on then, have this as well, I know you like this shit.' He said thrusting the book on palmistry into my hands as well. I was going to refuse but thought, *what the hell*. I stuffed the Tarot pack into one of the big pockets on my combat trousers and the palmistry book into the inside pocket of my leather jacket.

'Cheers.' I said. 'See you later.'

'See you, might pop round your gaff later.'

'Alright mate. Bye' I said, yanking the door open and making my way onto the landing. As I left I heard him take another toke on his pipe as he turned up the volume on his stereo.

- Three Wishes -

I made my way through the backstreets towards the beach, my pockets heavy with the stolen goods. Feeling a little guilty I placated myself by remembering that I had done it to stop my friend going to prison. I knew I had to break the cycle though - Terry would just keep trying the same trick till he or both of us got caught. I didn't imagine that the store would take long to notice the discrepancy between the missing books on the shelves and the shortfall of cash in their tills.

Reaching the beach I took a moment to take in a deep breath of the fresh sea air before heading home. The day had an unusual quality now, a thick mist clung to the sea making everything white, like an empty canvas waiting to be painted. The gong of the ornate clock tower indicated that it was three o'clock and I realized I'd better hurry back to wash my chef whites for work tomorrow.

As I walked along the esplanade, I noticed a figure emerging from behind the bus shelter. It was an old homeless lady who often heckled passersby, trying to make money anyway she could.

'Give ya a blowjob for a fiver.' She said with a croaky west country twang.

'You'd have to give me more than a fiver!' I said, laughing.

She looked at me vacantly. Her face a tapestry of lines and wrinkles, a large gold earring hanging from one ear.

I walked on with a smile on my face.

'Mark!' she suddenly commanded, a deep husk to her voice.

'How do you know my name?' I said, turning around to face her. Suddenly she was right there in my face, words spilling in a torrent from her cracked lips.

'Ando gav bi zhuklesko jal o pavori bi destesko.' She said, her voice *altered*. Her eyes, which I'm sure had been brown just a moment ago now looked at me *through* me, a pale *blue*.

'Excuse me?' I said.

'In the village without dogs the farmers walked without sticks. Ando gav bi zhuklesko shai piravel o manush bi destesko. In a village without a dog a man can walk without a stick.'

'Riiiight...' I said.

She grabbed my hand with bony fingers, peering intently into my face.

'You wish to escape the drugs which your friends force on you don't you? It's not your will, not your will.'

'Wha?'

'Shouldn't be here, not for you the kitchen of the damned' she laughed 'greater things in store, this is true. Yekka buliasa nashti beshes pe done grastende. With one behind you can't sit on two horses.'

'Look, I really must go.' I said sounding suddenly very English.

She grabbed onto my hand firmly and shook her head, eyes wide.

'Shhhhh!' she said, looking upwards and to the left with her scary eyes.

'Three things I tell you quick and true: One: You are good boy, but weak, Two: Those you call friends are parasites of the world. Three: A *worm* languishes within. Do not question these facts, I prove to you now that I speak Rrromany truth: Your father was a milkman, your mother a hairdresser. You wish to be more than you are and have been looking for a sign. Look at Time when tis short in the early hours. Nashti zhas vorta po drom o bango. You cannot walk straight when the road is bent.'

This avalanche cascaded out of the woman faster than I have ever heard a human being speak and I felt transfixed by her words, which were flavoured with a rich accent, the likes of which I had never heard before. But, the thing that really rooted me to the spot was that, interspersed with the seemingly nonsense words and phrases were clear fragments of truth. My father *was* a milkman and my mother *was* a hairdresser, she seemed to know about my friends too and the fact that I felt I didn't belong. Before I had a chance to respond she continued.

'One last truth I tell you.' She said.

Transfixed by those strange almost albino eyes, I could not speak.

'You fear the abyss.'

A shiver shot up my spine and my eyes went wide.

Still holding tightly to my hands she said: 'Reach into your pocket and you will find three coins - two, two, two.'

Reaching into my pocket with trembling hands I withdrew three two pound coins and stared at them in astonishment.

Before I knew what was happening, the gypsy grabbed hold of my other hand and closed it tightly over the coins.

'Te avel mange bakht drago mange wi te avav po gunoy. I give you three wishes one for each coin, now, think them in your mind and they will be. Choose now.'

'You're giving me three wishes?' I said, my voice very small.

'Say them in your *mind* and they will be! Anything but money, this I cannot grant. Number one!' she commanded.

I stood, perplexed.

'Number one!'

With everything I had heard I still found this difficult to swallow. 'Ok.' I said and absurdly, the first thing that came to mind was:

I want to be as strong as a lion.

'Two!' She said as if I had said this out loud.

To make ideas reality.

'Three!'

To live forever. I thought with a gasp.

A look of deep concentration appeared on the gypsy's face as she closed her eyes, her lips and eyelids quivering as she muttered something under her breath. She squeezed my hand even more tightly and then abruptly pushed it downwards before finally relinquishing her vice-like grip.

Feeling a little like the character at the end of *Ghostbusters* who inadvertently wishes for the *Stay puffed marshmallow man* to appear, I looked at the gypsy as she opened her eyes and looked down at my hand. I followed her gaze and, as I opened my clenched fist, she took the three coins that sat there.

'Zhan le Devlesa tai sastimasa.' She said and, turning back the way she came, began to walk off.

'Wait!' I shouted, shook up by the whole experience.

I jogged after her and, coming level as she turned back to look at me, I saw that her eyes had changed back to brown, the intensity gone, replaced with apathy.

'Can I help you love?' she said, her voice now possessing the usual west country twang.

'I...' I began to say.

She gave me a frightened look and continued walking.

Once again shocked and confused, I stood there for a long time and watched her slowly disappear into the white day.

- Spider's Web -

As the evening shadows crept over a purple sea, Terry and I sat and watched the town's humdrum activities dwindle. Ordinary people with ordinary lives clocked off from their nine to five; eager to be back in the welcoming womb of their homes. But I was happy to be right there with sea salt sharpening my senses and the taste of cherry wine dulling them. Remarkably, this was the second bottle for Terry that day, which was apparently essential - he had started to sober up. I took another swig of the thick warm liquid and Terry continued the largely one sided conversation:

'Seriously though Hems, we're like Knights you and me.'

'Eh?'

'We're the new knights, I mean look at that *vacuous* peasantry over there! They haven't got a fucking clue – they're gonna go home, watch *Eastenders*, go to sleep, wake up, go to work in their shitty lives and then repeat the whole pattern. We, on the other hand, are the bastions of our fates, masters of the Universe.'

'Like He-Man?'

'Fuck off Hems I'm serious! I was reading the I Ching last night and do you know what it said about you?'

'No, but I'm sure you're going to tell me.'

'Do you want to know or not?'

'No.'

'Fuck you then.'

'Alright tell me – what did the i-*thing* have to say about me?'

'The I-CHING! It allows you to draw a map of your future by using numerology and astrology. I used your date of birth and rising sign to do it. Basically *you're* fucked Hems, there's no money or girls or anything good for you until you're *old* when you have lots of metal in your chart.'

'Well that's reassuring.'

'Similar for me but the other way round, looks like I'm in store for some nice shiny metal in the form of the big bucks when I'm a young man Hems – Ker-*ching*!'

I wanted to tell him about my weird encounter with the old lady, to say, 'well *I'm* going to live forever!' but obviously this was ludicrous, so I decided to keep it to myself, at least for the time being until I had finished processing what had happened. Besides, he would just tell me I had been duped out of six quid and, the more I thought about it, the more I convinced myself that that was precisely what had happened. Instead, I took the bottle from Terry's hand and gave it a long swig.

'Oi, steady on Hems! Don't drink it all!' Terry said, snaring the bottle back.

I sat back with a sigh and as I did so, noticed a familiar figure walking towards us out of the mist.

'Oi Oi!' said Bob.

'Bainbury! Fucking hell man what are you doing here?'

'Need to score and Fudge is dry.'

'Oooh, shit? I've never known fudge to run out of weed – thought he was made of the stuff.'

'I know mate, I'm going to have to try Flint instead.'

'Flint? What, the guy who lives with Goodman? Oooh I don't know about him man. He's a bit of a psycho isn't he?'

'Well as long as he's got weed I don't give a shit – you coming?'

'Am I coming? Course I'm coming, you think I'm gonna sit and listen to Hems' shit all night?'

'Huh?' I said.

'Hurry up Hems.' Said Bob.

As the last vestiges of light were swallowed from the sky we made our way through the backstreets of Weymouth. This was always a bit of an adventure when slightly half cut, a feint magic seemed to line the streets as we passed from the sleepy veneer of the sea-front to the darker but somehow more real underworld concealed behind the tourist facade. Rows of houses here were owned by a notorious housing tycoon by the name of Conrob; a greedy, fat, swindling bastard who would screw his own grandmother out of her dole cheque, and probably had. As well as owning many of the properties in the area he was also a loan shark who preyed on the unfortunates who occupied his crumbling abodes. By letting out his *quality accommodation* to almost exclusively the down and out, wasted and weary, drug addicted masses of Weymouth who were pretty much guaranteed to require a financial *lending hand* to feed their habits, he secured a lucrative 40% interest from a legion of junkies every week. Of course, you can never trust a junkie to pay you what they owe, but as their landlord, Conrob had convinced these poor souls to have their dole cheques delivered to his office so that he could take out what they owed directly, and this was the true price of a loan. Every Thursday, the sunken eyed hordes would wait in line, snaking around the corner from Conrob's office where he dished out the pitiable sums that were left to them.

Reaching just one such Conrob house I noticed that one of the windows had been partially boarded up and it seemed that demolitions were still ongoing by the sound of the bickering couple inside. A soiled mattress lay on its side outside the house, propped up by a rotting sofa. It was as if we had been magically teleported to the early eighties and the set of *The Young Ones*.

Bob approached the front door and gave it three firm knocks. Possibly not the best way to knock on a dealer's door, as it's exactly how I imagined the police to knock.

After a moment the door was abruptly opened wide to reveal a thick set man with dreadlocks who looked down at Bob with the intensity of a pitbull.

'Is Flint in?' Bob said, adjusting his posture to match that of the unwelcoming door keeper.

'Who the fuck are you?'

'Who the fuck are *you*!?!' Bob retorted, once again adjusting his posture - standing forwards, head bowed, eyes of blue steel narrowly focussed into the eyes of the other.

Both men stood like that for what seemed like an eternity, neither willing to back down. But, just as I was starting to think that this might turn into a dangerous staring competition, the dreadlocked man threw the door wide and allowed us to step around him. He eyed us each carefully as we walked inside and I gave him a cheery 'hello', to which he narrowed his eyes.

Bob maintained his swagger, barging confidently up the stairs. There's one thing I will say about Bob, though he had his flaws, he also certainly had courage.

Three floors up and Bob pushed open the door into a large room that emanated an almost suffocating smell of skunk and josticks. We were immediately affronted by a second pitbull, but this time literally. The dog reared up on its hind legs and snarled and barked ferociously as we walked into the room. Bob and Terry staggered backwards slightly as the dog's owner struggled to hold onto its lead.

'Oi! Calm the fuck down!' Said the man, giving it a swift kick to the rear. The dog yelped but continued to growl as we edged further into the room, away from its yawning jaws. Looking around I could see that Flint was clearly making good business - the room was filled with people rolling joints or smoking them and in its centre sat a surprise: Spider. We knew Spider from Terry's previous residence where we had gotten stoned together on many occasions as he regaled us with tall tales of his textured past. Taking the opportunity to announce our presence and possibly jump the queue, Bob called out to him. 'Alright Spider!'

Spider looked up from his weighing scales and brushed long black hair from his face. Recognition registered as he scanned our faces.

'Alright boys' he said before resuming his task.

Moving forward through the small crowd we walked into the centre of the room.

'Where's Flint?' said Bob.

'Oh he's around here somewhere' said Spider weighing and cutting up what looked like a nine bar of dark brown *soap-bar*.

'What are you doing here? Haven't seen you for a while.'

'Just taking care of a bit of business,' said Spider, looking up with a broad smile on his face.

I had always liked Spider, he was intelligent, self assured and radiated an aura of calm. He was considerably older than us, in his fourties, and had earned all of our respect by appealing to different aspects of each of our personalities. Bob was impressed by his stories of running a large hydroponic farm, Terry by his unlikely claims of robbing banks and me simply by his small acts of kindness and apparently friendly nature. I wasn't aware that he was working with Flint and this might explain why other dealers in the area were apparently *dry*. In any case, this was good news for Bob.

'Sort us out an eighth mate.' Said Bob.

'No problem, here you go Bob, there's a juicy one right here with your name on it if you'll join me for a smoke?'

'Damn right mate.' Said Bob, loosening his belt and, with his back to the rest of the room, he put his hand down his trousers and retrieved a black felt pouch that he used to store his bong.

'Steady on mate, I mean, I know you like me and that...'

'Ha ha – I'm just getting me bong out in it!'

'Oh, so that's what you call it, arf arf.'

With his free hand, Bob took a ten and a five from his pocket and handed them to Spider, who casually opened a small red tin to reveal a large wad of notes and several bags of coins. Opening one of the bags he retrieved some coins and handed them to Bob along with the shiny brown package 'with Bob's name on it'.

'Thanks man.' Bob said and waited until Spider resumed his work of packaging the hash into various quantities before carefully examining his purchase.

Three of the stoners who had been sitting on the sofa got to their feet. 'We're off mate, thanks for the gear.'

'Oh, you're going already?'

'Gotta go and service the missus init!'

'Oh, well if you put it like that, give her one from me too!'

We all laughed as our fellow stoners made their exit, fortuitously leaving us a prime and comfortable position on the sofa, which we immediately took, much to the muted grumbling of others who had been sat on the floor.

'You been keeping your head down then Spider, you know old brassballs is gunning for you don't you? I'm guessing it's no coincidence that you and his prize thousand quid sound system disappeared on the same day?' said Terry, wanting a piece of the action.

Spider turned away and with his back turned said, 'Well Terence, between you and me, though of course I earnestly plead ignorance of any information pertaining to said sweet sound system theft, one thing that I *can* say is that whomever did perpetrate such a crime deserves a nice big smoke of top grade hashish.' There was a click, a flame and a deep intake of breath as Spider turned back to face us with a large spliff between his fingers and a broad smile on his face. He exhaled a large plume of white smoke that stung my eyes.

'You sly dog, Spider! Honestly though mate, that bloke is such a prick – the shit he gave you, he deserves worse.'

'Indeed. Anyway, what you boys been up to? You alright there, Mr Hems? Here get your chops round this.'

I took the joint and took a quick toke. 'Cheers mate. Yeah, not bad, just had a bit of a drink on the beach.'

'Hems!' Terry said, nudging me and passing me a hot pipe.

'I'm alright with this thanks Terry.'

'Hems!' he repeated, this time poking me hard in the rib cage. I took the pipe as Terry lit the bowl and I inhaled until the hash was white.

'So how did you end up working with Flint, Spider?' I said as Terry busied himself building another pipe.

'Long story short, I needed a place to stay and Mr Flint offered to help me out in exchange for a little help with a supply and demand problem.'

'Ah, say no more.' I said. Spider had once disclosed to us that he had a couple of friends up north looking after his *assets* for him after his hydroponic operation had been busted. Maybe his tall tales weren't so tall after all. I still didn't believe his talk of bank robberies though...

Bob handed me his bong. I really didn't want to take another hit right now but I also didn't want to look like a lightweight, particularly not in a room of hardened tokers. I handed Spider his spliff and took a toke on Bobs bong. The water bubbled as I inhaled a potent lungful of smoke and nearly coughed as I held it in for a moment. Before exhaling I felt my mind reel as it tried to cope with the heady mixture of pot and wine that I had consumed. Control started to slip as I handed the bong to Spider.

'No thanks Mark – I prefer the spliffage.'

I offered the bong to Terry who finished loading his pipe and took the bong from my hands. I was glad to be rid of it as I sunk back into the sofa and looked around the room. There were a couple of people playing *Wipeout* on playstation and I became entranced by the trails of blue light that danced across the screen.

'Hems.' Said Terry once again thrusting his pipe into my hands. No longer possessing the will to refuse and wanting to avoid another poke to the ribs, I took the pipe and inhaled once more before flopping backwards on the sofa and closing my eyes.

'There goes Hemsy!' said Bob.

I opened my eyes and smiled at him before closing them again.

My reverie was immediately shattered when the dog began to snarl as a newcomer entered the room followed by a gust of cold air. I heard the dog once again give a sharp 'Yip!' as it received another kick and Flint entered the room. I sat up straight, not wanting to appear disrespectful in the dealer's home. Approaching us, he looked us over distrustfully. He did *not* look happy.

'The fucking stash has gone!'

Spider looked at him with a perplexed expression. 'It's *here* man' he said, pointing to a large brown slab on the table.

'The *main* fucking stash! It's gone!'

'What? Shit I thought Pete was looking after it.'

At that moment the heavy set man who had let us in burst through the door pointing his finger at Spider.

'It's that *cunt*! I told you we shouldn't trust him!'

He marched over to Spider and shouted in his face, 'You've had it haven't you, you cunt!'

Calmly, Spider put down his spliff and said quietly to the man: 'Call me that again and you'll be struggling to hold your insides together after I kick your sorry arse through that window.'

The heavy looked astounded. 'CUNT!' he shouted in Spider's face.

Before anyone knew what was happening, Spider leaped to his feet and in one fluid motion kicked high into the man's throat, forcing him backwards towards the open window. He would have gone through it too, if not for the dog. Wanting to be part of the commotion, the pitbull had broken free of its owners clutches and ran into the line of the flailing man's doomed trajectory towards the window, tripping him up so that he fell just short of certain death.

The room went silent as Spider sat back down, took a deep toke on his joint and continued his work. Calmly, he turned his gaze towards Flint who was still standing slack jawed.

'Flint, as you can see I have been sat here sorting out a bunch of your punters since you saw me this morning. I promise you that I did not steal your stash and I feel quite insulted that you would even *think* that after setting you up with the deal in the first place.'

Flint looked at him, his face a confused mixture of shock and anger. 'Alright' he paused, 'well I'm going to find out who's done this and I'm gonna' he began to shout 'fucking *cut* em up! What the fuck you looking at?'

I nearly had a heart attack as I realised he was talking to me and I simply raised my hands, unable to speak. Fortunately he headed for the door, barging past a girl who had been painting her nails, forcing her to paint a slash of pink over her toes.

'Hey!' she cried and Flint turned back briefly to push his palm in her face, forcing her head against the wall so that she yelped in pain. Exiting the room he slammed the door hard behind him and pounded down the stairs. The heavy was still finding his feet and had to ward off the dog as it snarled in his face. Clearly shook up, he went after his friend.

The room went quiet and I asked the girl with the oddly painted toes if she was ok. With mascara streaked cheeks she nodded and stifled a sob. I looked at Spider and he was completely unperturbed by events - as if nothing had happened. I wondered at my earlier assessment of him, his age and skinny appearance completely belied the ability he had demonstrated in dealing with the dreadlocked heavy, a big man who I certainly would *not* wish to mess with. He was a collection of contradictions and this made me question the trust I had placed in him. Having said this, maybe he had always been honest with us, indeed, he had always claimed, amongst other things, to be an ex paratrooper and when combined with the other tales of bank robbery and drug operations I had disbelieved him, but what if he had been telling the truth all along? This would certainly go some way to explaining his apparent calm, lightning fast reactions and physical prowess in the heat of such a frankly terrifying exchange.

'You alright there Mr Hems?' He said to me, seeming to penetrate my soul with his black spider eyes.

'Of course, why shouldn't I be?' I said and laughed nervously.

'Well, let's get back to the caning of this fine resin then shall we?' he said handing me another joint.

- Tapeworms and Werewolves -

As we continued to smoke I sank deeper and deeper into the sofa. I was utterly *stoned* and for the last hour I had been unable to open my eyes, once again prey to a legion of nightmare thoughts and paranoid delusions. Fortunately nobody noticed as the darkness in the room concealed my helpless state.

'We gotta shoot man.' Said Bob rising off the sofa with Terry in tow.

Spider looked up at them and smiled. 'Ok boys, take it easy.'

I felt Terry's eyes on me. 'You coming Hems?'

I shivered as I struggled against the nausea that had been produced by the concoction of pot, wine and fear. 'I'm going to stay a bit longer' I managed to say, afraid to get up lest I be sick and humiliate myself.

'You sure, Hems?' Bob said, and I nodded in response before once again closing my eyes.

Bob looked at Terry and they shrugged before shaking Spider's hand and making their way to the door.

As they left, the girl with the painted toes assumed Terry's position on the sofa next to me with one of her friends.

'You alright mate?' she said.

I looked up at her and nodded before letting my head loll back onto my shoulder.

'Right, let's see what's on the box...' said Spider walking over to the TV. A cacophony of noise enveloped my consciousness. I didn't know whether the TV was obscenely loud or whether my drug addled mind was amplifying the volume, but to me it was a juggernaut of noise that fried my already frazzled nerves.

Spider flicked through a couple of channels before settling on *Eastenders* and my mind presented the scene of the *Queen Vic Pub* as two brothers spoke in thick cockney accents:-

'Slow down Grant, who did this?'

'That fuckin double crossing bastard, he's been playing both sides.'

'Whoa, slow down, what do you mean, who are you talking about?'

'Spider bruv!'

Spider?

'What do you mean – playing both sides?'

'Well I've just had a very interesting little conversation with a dealer named Fudge who claims that Spider had kindly offered to set him up with a right Brucy Bonus shipment, care of his contacts up north.'

What the hell?

'Hold on, you saying he's been selling to both of us?'

'Nah, there's more, he delivered the shipment alright but then buggered off with both the merch *and* the money!'

'And I would bet your life that that's the self same shipment that he helpfully sold to us.'

'Double crossing snake! Ha ha, but one man's loss is another man's gain eh?'

'Not when the bastards gone and robbed ours an all it isn't!'

'What?! Tell me you're joking! I'm going to...'

Spider changed the channel and I was transported from a bustling pub to what sounded like a dark forest judging by the rustling of wind through trees – I was still unable to open my eyes. An owl hooted loudly and an organ began playing chilling minor keys. The voice of an elderly lady, who instantly reminded me of the gypsy, echoed through the darkness of my mind.

'Never go into the woods alone at night.

'I won't Grandma.' echoed the voice of a child, but judging by the rustling of the wind through the leaves and the sound of small branches crunching underfoot- that's precisely what she seemed to be doing. The abrupt sound of a howl in the distance frightened me with its sheer volume and sent a shiver down my spine. *Why was the television so loud?* I needed to get out of here, but felt rooted to the spot. For some reason I was terrified. Irrationally I felt that even the slightest movement would result in death and had an odd sense of foreboding.

The old lady's voice rang in my mind again, 'There are terrible things in those woods, they don't like the daylight, but come out at night...'

My mind conjured the image of a dark grey room with a large operating table standing in the middle. The chilling music seemed to amplify this scene as I focussed on what lay on the table. It was a ghostly white, naked man. He was slightly obscured by another man in a white coat – presumably a doctor - who appeared to be struggling with something. I looked more closely and saw that he was attempting to yank something from the man's mouth with a pair of enormous pliers. As I looked on with curiosity, more men were revealed. One was holding the man's mouth open with what appeared to be metal rods and another held pliers like the first. I looked down at the ghostly white man's face but it was too dark to make out his features.

But what I did see horrified me.

There was something terrible emerging from his mouth. Something *black*. As I looked on in horror, unable to avert my mind, I saw that it was the head of an enormous worm!

A shiver went up my spine as a shrill metallic noise reverberated around the room and suddenly the gypsy woman appeared. *'A WORM LANGUISHES WITHIN!'* She cried, and as the men in white coats heaved with their tools, the worm slithered further out of the man's mouth to reveal its enormous length. It had to be ten feet long! My mind reeled and just as I thought I could bear no more, the worm began to thrash, spraying blood from the poor host's ruptured face as it slithered out of his mouth.

Whilst the white coats struggled with the gigantic creature, I looked away in horror and focussed on the man on the table. As I watched in horror he began to tremble. *He's alive!*

Slowly, he began to turn his face towards me and with abject horror I finally recognised my own face looking back at me. He opened his mouth wider than humanly possible and issued a blood curdling scream as his face collapsed.

Snapping my eyes wide open, my body seemed to explode in a frenzy of terrified nervous energy as my dinner erupted in a hot torrent all over the carpet of one of the most dangerous drug dealers in the country.

'What the FUCK!?' To my dismay it was Flint's voice – he must have returned whilst I lay prey to my waking nightmare.

'I'm sorry', I blurted, wondering how much terror I could take but feeling slightly better due to the evacuation of what felt like poison and a massive injection of adrenaline.

'I'm going to fuck you up!' said Flint making his way in my direction.

'I'll clean it up' I said immediately, moving away from him towards the kitchen.

Perhaps calculating that if he did 'fuck me up' there would be no one left to clean up the mess, Flint hesitated as he watched me frantically searching for a cloth. I moved with the speed of a man possessed, feeling that my life may well be at risk. I found a cloth, a washing bowl and some detergent and quickly filled up the bowl with hot water. I returned to the floor and immediately began scrubbing my stinking mess, not wanting to look up at Flint.

'Shall I give him a kick said Flint's flatmate, Goodman.

'Hold on, wait till he's done.'

I continued scrubbing and prayed that I was doing a good job.

'What the fuck? There's weird shit in your sick man!'

I looked up at him and he was prodding a small puddle of my sick with a spoon. He looked at me squarely with dark eyes and fury seemed to have been replaced with fascination. Shovelling up some of the noxious pink muck, he put the spoon under my nose and said something that scared me worse than a beating:

'You've got tapeworms mate.'

With mounting horror I looked at the mushroom like segments on the spoon and struggled to contain a second wave of nausea.

- The Lion the Witch and the Beast -

In an attempt to erase the knowledge that I had been harbouring within me a disgusting parasite, and to avoid being beaten to death, I scrubbed fervently at the carpet until all possible evidence of what had occurred was eliminated.

'Are you gonna stand for that shit, Flint?' Goodman was still trying to goad Flint into dishing out a beating.

'Shut up, Goodman.'

I completed my task and emptied the bowl into the sink, ensuring that I washed the sink as thoroughly as the carpet. I was feeling fully alert with adrenaline still coursing through my veins and just wanted to get out of this nightmare. I walked over to Flint and once again apologized.

'Yeah, just fuck off.' Flint said, returning his gaze to the TV - now disinterested. Picking up my coat I had to stifle a nervous shiver. I looked at the girl with the painted toes who had now moved to the other side of the room and regarded me with disgust. Without saying anything more I walked to the door and had one more obstacle to overcome. The pitbull guarded my exit. It stood with it's heckles raised ready to pounce. As I approached, it began to snarl, but I was not going to hesitate for a moment to escape this nightmare. Without breaking my stride, I approached the dog and held his eyes. He abruptly stood up and began to bark ferociously. Still moving forwards I thrust my finger towards the floor.

'SSSIT!' I said in the most commanding voice I could muster.

The dog sat down.

Astonished but not wasting a moment, I walked around the now whimpering mutt, drew back the hefty bolt and exited the drug den. I ran down the stairs and out of the building as fast as my fragile body would allow, and, fearful that Flint might change his mind and come after me, continued running out into the night and through the backstreets. I didn't stop until I reached the sea front and the relative safety of the bright lights of the esplanade. My heart was beating fast and despite the coldness of the night air I was sweating. The wind gusted light rain into my face and I was thankful for it, thankful at managing to survive relatively unscathed.

Unscathed?

My mind taunted me with the image of my naked body and the giant worm and then, like a before and after shot in a detergent advert, juxtaposed the grey sections of worm that Flint had discovered in my vomit.

You've got tapeworm's mate.

It was if my mind had made the nightmare real. I thought back to the gypsy woman and shuddered - my first wish had been to *make ideas into reality*. Could it be that my wish had come true? No - the gypsy was surely just a con woman. But the things she had *known*.

Maybe it was simply my subconscious revealing a secret that I already knew on some level. I certainly wasn't aware of the fact on a conscious level and maybe the worms weren't even there?

In my mind's eye I pictured the worms on the spoon and felt sick again. I suppose it was possible that I could have imagined them. But Flint had *seen* them! This was a fact that I could not deny, there was no possible way that he could have known the private nightmare that I had suffered unless he was some kind of psychic. That I doubted. Psy*cho* maybe, but psy*chic,* unlikely.

The vision of my own screaming face flooded into my mind and I shuddered as I looked at the raging sea. The wind was blowing hard and as I started to walk along the esplanade towards my house I got the sense that dark figures in the water followed me, whispering.

That was the last thing I wanted to imagine, especially if my wish had come true.

I shivered again and decided to run but as I did so, the wind seemed to increase in intensity and the whispering became louder until I was sure it was chanting my name. I didn't dare look back as I was sure that I would see crowds of the walking dead baying for my soul.

Reaching my house, which overlooked the beach, I struggled to find my keys and for a moment I thought that I might have left them at Flint's house. Terrified I looked back at the beach and could have sworn that there were swathes of shadowy figures moving towards me. Then, with no small measure of relief, my hand chanced upon the metal of my keys. Nearly fumbling them out of my pocket, I unlocked the door and wrenched it wide, virtually throwing myself inside. As I closed the door behind me, I chanced a furtive glance back to the beach.

There was nothing there.

Relieved to be back in the house I turned around and was confronted by a looming figure.

'Arrggh!' I screamed.

'Whoa there, you scared the crap out of me!' Said Malcolm, my mild mannered next door neighbour.

'Sorry Malcolm, I thought you were someone else.'

'Jesus! Who were you expecting? Satan and all of his minions by the looks of it!'

'Something like that.' I said, still getting my breath back.

He shrugged. 'Oh well, have a good evening, I'm going to watch my cars.'

I stood on the stairs for a moment to allow my heart to swing back into its natural rhythm and then made my way to my room, berating myself for getting so carried away. It had been one hell of a day.

I opened the door to my flat and quickly closed the door on the frightening world I had left behind. Then I collapsed onto the bed, glad to have survived and comforted by the familiar smell of josticks.

I lay there for a long time, just mulling things over in my mind until a knock on the door shook me out of my slumber. I looked at the alarm clock by the side of my bed and the red digits shone back, 2:22.

Three Two's for three wishes.

A bit late for anyone to be making a social visit, I thought. What if it was Flint? What if he thought that I was the one who had stolen his weed?

'Mark?' A familiar female voice.

'Teresa?'

'Yeah, it's me.'

What was Teresa doing here at this time? I didn't even know she knew where I lived. Teresa was a girl I had had something of a crush on in High school despite the fact that she was way out of my league. We were quite good friends now and I hung out with her from time to time at college.

I opened the door and looked into the face of a blonde haired angel. Beautiful big blue eyes with long lashes peered up at me. 'Can I come in?'

'Of course.' I said opening the door and stepping aside so that she could enter. I quickly scanned the room hoping that the room wasn't in a state and was relieved that I was a tidy person.

Teresa walked into the room and sat on the rumpled bed sheets.

'Is everything ok?' I asked, looking at her with concern.

'I just needed someone to talk to that's all.'

Sitting on the bed next to her I asked, 'What's up?'

'Me and John have split up again.'

'Oh, I'm sorry T.'

She started to cry and I put my arm around her.

'Shhhhhh.' I said soothingly, enjoying the warmth of her body and the scent of her hair. She hugged me close and I got a strong whiff of white musk – probably my favourite smell in the world.

'You know' I began 'I don't know what he did but he must be a complete idiot to not realise what he has in you.'

She stopped sobbing for a moment and looked up at me with moist eyes, her make up running.

'What *does* he have in me?' she asked.

I hadn't really thought this through but damn the consequences, this was a girl I had been very much in love with for years.

'Well, let me see, you're gorgeous, smart, funny...'

She suddenly planted her mouth against mine and I breathed in hot, sweet breath. *Was this really happening?* Almost in answer, she stroked my face and caressed my tongue with hers. I began to feel aroused, I had imagined this moment for a long time and now that it was finally happening it was bliss. She began to unbutton my shirt and as I caressed her ample breasts, a small sigh escaped her.

'Make love to me' she whispered, continuing to unbutton my shirt. I feared that my erection would tear through my jeans as she brushed her fingers over my crotch playfully before removing my shirt. Exposing my chest she brought pearly white thighs up around my body and placed her palms on my chest. I had never wanted anybody so badly in all of my life as I put my hands around her neck and kissed her deeply. She sat up and threw her head back, sumptuous blond hair gracefully flowing backwards as she pushed down harder on my chest and her hands sank beneath my... *skin*! Alarmed, I looked at her hands and they were indeed pushing down into my flesh. I gasped and tried to push her up but she was so *strong*! Suddenly I became quite panicked and was about to ask her to stop when I looked into her eyes. No longer the eyes of a beautiful young woman - they had transformed into the albino eyes of the old gypsy! Then, as I struggled to pull her hands from within me, a snout and enormous teeth tore through the flesh of her face.

I screamed as I tried to avoid gnashing teeth - thick spittle flying in all directions. The pressure heaving down on my chest was now enormous and as I looked down I saw to my horror that my chest cavity was actually *crumbling* in on itself as if it were made of sand. I watched helplessly as my skin cracked and shrivelled, the colour sapped grey as the Teresa creature pushed ever deeper, sucking up my very life force. My heart struggled under the immense pressure and I once again looked into her face to reveal those albino eyes, laughing at me.

'Noooooo!' I cried, my body now little more than a desiccated husk. I felt my teeth falling out and the skin of my face tightening around my skull. I closed my eyes, almost accepting the end and once again encountered the abyss inside my mind, my ethereal body hurtling towards death. But I knew the abyss. I *knew* how to defeat it. I was not going to relinquish my life to this nightmare.

'Up!' I cried, 'Up! Up! Up!'

And with the words I felt my body begin to firm up against the pressure of the apparition's claws. I pushed outwards with my mind in all directions, and out of the remnants of my collapsed chest, powerful muscles began to emerge. I felt the beast begin to withdraw with surprise as my body began to radiate a golden light. I looked down at myself to reveal a new body, *the body of a lion*! The beast withdrew her clawed hands and looked at me, shock clearly apparent on her now hideous features. I had transformed into something half lion, half man and felt enormous power flowing through me. I began to rise off the bed, golden light obliterating the room so that only white remained. Recovering from the apparent shock, the beast launched itself at me and I dodged out of the way but grabbed it's still golden hair, using its momentum to swing it through the air. A high pitched shriek issued from the creature as I swung it in wide arcs around my head. I felt that I had harnessed some kind of immense energy and it felt wonderful. My senses were super attuned to every movement. I let go of the creature's hair and she flew through the air, shrieking as she connected with something before slumping to the floor with a *crunch*.

I looked down at the creature, now pitiful and shrunken, and it began to laugh a terrible laugh.

I felt my confidence waver and shadows began to creep into the white world, revealing a dark night. Realizing suddenly that I had flown high into the sky I began to fall and looked down to reveal the houses of Weymouth far below me. As I fell, the creature continued to laugh until the laughter became unbearably loud, suffocating my senses. I plummeted towards the ground and my heart once more creaked under the strain as the beast leapt towards me.

I awoke with a start - sweat pouring from my body, my heart pounding in my chest. Early morning light poured in through cracks in the curtains and seagulls cawed.

I let my head fall back on the pillow and sighed with relief. *Just a dream.*

- Hot Shower -

Dragging myself out of bed I stood and looked in the mirror half expecting to be confronted with the desiccated husk I had become in the dream. Remarkably I didn't look too bad considering the previous night's excesses, but felt a lot worse than I looked. My head swam with fragments of disturbing memories - the enormous tapeworm, albino eyes that should have been brown and the Teresa-creature.

Then I remembered making the pitbull sit down on command and a small laugh escaped me. With the smile still lingering on my face I looked at the alarm and realized that I was late for work.

Shit!

Discarding all of the previous day's events from my mind, I ran back to the sink, picked up my toothbrush and began speed brushing. Gargling some water I simultaneously splashed water in my face and combed my hair back before spitting out minty water. Deciding that I didn't have enough time to make myself look a million dollars, I jumped over the bed and snared my chef whites from where they hung on the windowsill. Dry, well *almost*. The hang-outside-the-window-until-dry method wasn't as effective in October as it was in July, but they'd dry off soon enough in the hot kitchen. After putting on my chefs checks, I slipped on a slightly pink t-shirt which used to be white, stepped into my trainers and off I went.

I was already ten minutes late but fortunately I lived literally next door to work, so running down the stairs and out of the door I encountered a bracing sea breeze before opening the door to the *Crows Nest* restaurant.

It would have been a handsome looking building in its day, indeed, despite looking a bit weathered it still had its charms. It was part of a sweeping line of Georgian buildings that overlooked the seafront on one side and the town on the other – ideally placed to grab the attention of the hungry masses of Weymouth. Bus loads of pensioners were drawn to the easy-to-chew cottage pies, and families on a budget were attracted by the promise of a free children's meal for every adult meal ordered. Plus, the kids loved it - it had been decorated in a pirate theme with each of the walls telling the story of a sea battle or a ship at harbour or pirates counting their treasure. There were even nets hanging from parts of the ceiling and old fashioned oil lanterns hung here and there.

As I entered, the *Duchess* gave me a sour look and pointed vigorously at her watch. 'Mark, you're twelve minutes late!' she said in a shrill voice that went straight through me.

'I know, I'm sorry – I overslept.' I hurried down the stairs as much to avoid the harlot as to clock in for my shift. Opening the door to the cellar I picked out my clock card and dropped it into the slot at the top of the hole-punch machine. A *'kerchunk'* later and I was jogging back up the stairs and over the guard rail. Walking past the Duchess - who was actually just the manageress and *not* a real duchess - I kept my eyes down and made my way hastily up the stairs. Reaching the top I inputted my pass code and made my way into the kitchen.

Here began my daily routine:

Lights, check.

Power levers, cranked.

Fryers, on.

Range, lit.

Saucepans, filled with water.

Peas in steamer.

Soup in microwave. 5 minutes.

Slop of soup on already stained t-shirt. Slight improvement.

Next?

Today was Monday, which meant that it was the head chef's day off and it was down to me to set up the self service section and restaurants with enough food to see them through the day. Fortunately for me I only had to get through two and a half hours before I could grab a half hour break and some much needed coffee and breakfast. For a moment I wondered why I was so hungry then remembered throwing up the night before. It all seemed like a horrible dream now, in the morning light.

Right, next were the potatoes. I grabbed a twenty five pound sack from the store room and hoisted it over to the rumbler, a large steel contraption with a spinning base responsible for skinning the potatoes and carrots. Tearing the sack open with a knife, I lifted the potatoes onto my shoulder and allowed a good number of them to fall into the spinning metal belly of the rumbler. Once I had skinned three bags, I transferred the potatoes to large buckets of water, ready to be boiled.

After washing the rumbler of potato muck, I carried out the same procedure with a bag of carrots and while they were rumbling away, I headed into the pastry room to make the pies. Six steak and kidney pies should do it, followed by the topping of four enormous cottage pies.

Shit! I'd forgotten to put the other pies in the oven. Rushing into the fridge I picked up two steak and kidney pies and hurried over to the oven, which I had forgotten to turn on.

'Fuck!'

I opened the enormous doors of the oven which triggered the starting mechanism, then, reaching over the range I lit a taper and subsequently brought the steel leviathan to life. After quickly stocking the oven with pies I checked my watch. Damn, I had lost another ten minutes with that mistake.

Next was the beef, which I *should* have put in first! Then the pork, then two cottage pies.

Shit the carrots!

I ran over to the rumbler and turned the power off. Already I could see a thick orange mush flowing out of the dispatch door. Gingerly lifting off the lid I observed that most of the carrots had now been miniaturised, with the rest of them transformed into the orange mush. I would have to take the thing apart to unblock the pipes, which would lose me even more time. Things were not going well.

Slowly, opening the dispatch door a fraction to get rid of some of the excess mush, I turned the machine back on, braced against the weight of the carrots against the door and slowly opened it some of the way to let the carrots filter through into the sink. That was the plan anyway. Unfortunately a multitude of carrots rushed through the door, into the sink full of water and sludge, water and said sludge splashing big splodges all over my now multi-coloured T-shirt.

Looking at my watch I saw that it was ten o'clock and I had earned a measly three pounds seventy pence. *Kerching!* Maybe Terry's i-*thing* was right! I chuckled to myself as I began disassembling the mammoth machine.

When eleven o'clock finally came I was already exhausted. Unfortunately, because I was a bit behind, I had to continue to work for another half an hour to make sure that everything was ready for the upstairs restaurant opening at twelve. Roger arrived as I was giving the finishing touches to the dish of the day - a tasty looking lamb hotpot. Succulent pieces of lamb stewed in a rich gravy with mushrooms, onions, carrots and peas and a generous helping of mint sauce, topped with crispy golden potato slices.

'Good moaning' said Roger as he appeared from nowhere. 'Something smells good'.

Roger was a big fella who made for quite a reliable kitchen hand with a sturdy no nonsense attitude towards work. He was one of a long line of cooks that had typically not been able to hack the heat, low pay and lousy hours demanded of the job.

'Morning Rodge.' I said, dusting my hotpots with rubbed parsley.

Roger surveyed the kitchen before looking me up and down.

'Don't ask mate, let's just say I haven't had the best morning.'

'Ha, well you'd better not let the Duchess see you like that – she's gunning for you already.'

'Why, what did she say?'

'Oh, something along the lines of that Hems character coming in late *again.'*

'Ha, whatever.'

'So, you going on break?'

'Yeah, just got a few things to finish off first, but if you could take care of the beef and the cabbage, that would be cool.'

'Ai ai captain.'

Finishing up my hotpots I loaded up the trolley with two steaming steak and kidney pies and a large cottage pie, wheeled it over to the lift and wished it farewell on its journey to the self service section of the restaurant. Next was the sweet.

Upon finally getting caught up I went downstairs to make myself a well deserved breakfast. The place was now in full swing with a small queue of punters waiting in line to order.

Grimesy, the general manager was on duty today. At sixty years old he was the Crows Nest's longest serving member and was responsible for the self service section as well as all manner of repair and maintenance jobs throughout the building.

'Morning Grimesy!' I said, squeezing past him between the hot plates and the griddle as he flipped an egg onto a plate.

'Maximus!' He said. This was his nickname for me, ever since watching *Gladiator*. He would often follow this with *Ornelius, Cornelius, Flavius* and any other made up Roman name he could think of before I would often reply in my best Russell Crowe impersonation:

'Father to a murdered son, husband to a murdered wife, and I *will* have my breakfast in this life or the next!'

'Possibly the next life if you don't get a move on.' He said with a wink.

I skirted past him as he turned round to apply two sausages to two plates of work in-progress-breakfasts.

This was easily the best part of the day, the smell of bacon, sausages and egg still appealed even after working with the smells of food for years.

I cracked an egg onto the griddle and mashed it up like a mini omelette before making my way to the hotplate to dish out a juicy rasher of bacon and a fat sausage. Peering above the counter I checked for any signs of the Duchess before surreptitiously scooping a generous portion of mushrooms onto my plate and hiding them underneath some beans. There was a very strict policy on staff meals and mushrooms weren't allowed because they were expensive. Sod it, on the wage I was on with the sometimes spirit crushing work I had to do I felt more than justified in taking the occasional small liberty.

I looked over at Grimesy who noticed my illegal helping of mushrooms but winked at me anyway, so I continued to shovel my mini omelette off the griddle and onto my plate to completely cover my contraband. He was a good old sort, Mr Grimes and, when the owners weren't around, he too had his own small liberties and would often indulge in a glass of red wine or two when charged with the night shift. It was good for the constitution, apparently.

Picking up my plate and mug and making my way back around the counter I noticed that the new waitress was getting a grilling from the Duchess – presumably for not folding the napkins in the proper fashion or something. I gave the waitress an exaggerated look as if to say *Oh my god it's the end of the world* and she stifled an awkward smile before turning her gaze quickly back to her commanding chief.

Looking outside I judged that it was a little too nippy so decided to sit in the quiet seating area downstairs that was currently cordoned off – we mainly only used this place in the summer when the whole place would fill up. Three floors of bustling chaos. Today though it was tranquil and I could do with a bit of peace and quiet. Carefully stepping over the cordon I went downstairs and sat at my usual seat before digging in heartily to my morning spoils.

The basement was done up like a pirate cavern, the walls covered with gleaming gold treasure and peg legged pirates. Some of the pirates even had an uncanny resemblance to the crew of the Crows Nest - there was Grimesy wearing a bandana and counting gold coins,

Roger wearing a pirate hat and sharpening his sword and the head chef, Simon, standing watch with his hand on a cutlass. The resemblance really was uncanny, which was all the more surprising because it had been painted in the early eighties long before these people, with the exception of Grimesy, had started work there. The absence of my own likeness was reassuring as I felt - and hoped - that I was destined for greater things than spending my days covered in carrot sludge and soup. Then I thought back to the Gypsy lady again. S*houldn't be here, not for you the kitchen of the damned*.

Later that day, having survived a modest lunchtime rush I remembered that I had promised to clean the large fryer. This was *not* a nice job. As Roger busied himself cutting cabbage as part of the preparations for the next day, I switched off the fryer and brought over an empty oil can to sit at its base.

Red Hot Chili Peppers, *Californication* album was playing on the stereo, and, as one of our favourite songs, *Other Side* came on, Roger turned it up to eleven.

'Good man!' I said, placing a large funnel into the top of the oil can and lining it up to catch the oil that I would release from the outlet valve on the fryer. Assessing that everything was as it should be, I tugged at the outlet valve and almost slipped on the greasy floor, which perfectly mirrored the lyrics to the song which I sang:

'How long, how lo-o-ong can I *slide*...'

Noticing my short trip across the floor, Roger laughed as I readjusted my posture and tried again. It was a tough bugger and was slightly bent so you really had to pull. Getting a better grip, I pulled hard. With a pop, the lever sprang back and bubbling hot oil chugged into the funnel and into the oil can. Watching the oil go down I continued to sing: 'Take it on the other side – take it on the other side...'

Then in unison Roger and I threw out our arms and sang. 'How long, how lo-o-ng will I *sliiiide* and separate my si-i-i-ide, I don't, I don't believe it's baaaaa-a-ad, slitting my throat is all I ever...'

Smiling to myself, I returned to my task and with the oil now nearly emptied from the fryer, I went to the sink to fill up a large plastic container with soapy water with which to zap the crusty grease. All of the oil had now drained away and was bubbling away in the oil can where it would cool. Then, just as I was about to close the outlet valve on the fryer so that I could start washing the inside of it, the telephone rang.

I stopped what I was doing and picked up the phone. 'Crows Nest', I said in my phone voice.

'Taylor's' said the clipped voice of the Duchess.

'Ok.' I said and heard the click that signified that the call was being diverted to an outside line.

'Hello?'

'Hello, Taylor's to take your order?' said the voice of what I imagined to be a burly bearded butcher.

'Yep.' I said, reaching to pick up the order that the head chef had written down the previous day.

'We would like...' I said surveying the order. 'Three joints of topside, two joints of pork, fifteen pounds of diced chuck, ten pounds of mince, ten eight ounce rump steaks and three gammon steaks please.'

'Is that everything?' said the butcher.

'That's everything.' I said.

'Ok, thanks very much, we'll see you tomorrow.'

'Ok, thanks, bye.' I said returning the phone to its cradle and the pad to the top of the microwave.

Now, where was I?

Looking back at the fryer I remembered what I was doing and dipped a scourer into the soapy water to resume my cleaning job. Jeez it was amazing how dirty these things got. The inside of the fryer was lined with a thick covering of crusty, thick yellow oil. I poured water from the container against the sides and stepped back a little as hot steam rose from the metal giant. There was a knack with this job - I found that if you poured the water onto the sides whilst washing them with the scourer - and sometimes a wall paper scraper - the hard oil scraped away relatively easily.

I had poured about half of the container of water into the mouth of the fryer when I became aware of a chugging noise at my feet. Looking down I noticed that hot steam was emanating from the top of the oil can and with horror it dawned on me that I had forgotten to close the outlet valve on the fryer. This meant that all of the soapy water that I had poured into the fryer had travelled down, through the open valve, into the funnel and into a gallon of hot bubbling oil!

Everything slowed down then. The oil can began to dance from side to side as the pressure of the competing elements encased within it forced torrents of oil to erupt from its mouth. I began to move out of the way and shouted to Roger to get back. Shocked by the sudden activity, Roger turned around to look at me before looking past me at the chugging catastrophe that was about to happen.

Having nowhere else to go, the entire contents of the oil can spewed into the air - a fountain of destruction. Hitting the ceiling with force and rebounding in all directions, I watched in horror as it covered the walls all around me.

'JESUS CHRIST!' said Roger, his mouth an 'O' of awe and fear. He had managed to get out of the way just in time but I stood right in the line of fire.

Roger looked at me, then looked at the wall behind me, then looked back at me.

'What?' I said.

'Are you alright?' He said, a frown etched into his forehead.

'I think so', I said, looking around in shock.

Hot oil still dripped down from the ceiling.

I looked behind me and it was running down the wall. Then I looked down at myself, expecting to feel the pain of first degree burns as they gnawed through the shock, but I didn't have a spot of oil on me. Not a spot. I looked at my hands, which seemed ok so I carefully felt my face, hot and wet with the heat, but seemingly unharmed. I ran my hands up and down my arms, inspecting them. Nothing. I checked my legs, again nothing.

'Somebody up there must love you.' said Roger, still assessing my position directly between the dripping wall and the still steaming oil can.

'Yeah.' I said, too stunned to say more.

'Better get this cleaned up, I suppose.' Said Roger heading for a mop.

'Yeah.' I said, unable to move.

A loud noise shattered my stunned reverie as the plastic funnel fell off the top of the oven where it had landed.

'Yeah.' I repeated to myself.

The next twenty minutes was spent mopping the ceiling and the walls. Never in my life did I imagine having to mop a ceiling. Not the nicest job in the world. As I dragged the mop across the main patch of oil, drops of water, oil and strands of mop fell down on me to really top off my day. The last thing I needed at that moment was for the Duchess to come snooping around, but unfortunately that's exactly what happened.

'Mark! What on earth are you doing!' she shrieked.

'Oh, erm, just er had a bit of time to kill so thought I'd give the ceiling a bit of a spruce up, you know?'

'No, I *don't* know actually, Mark. What's been going on *here*?!' she looked around the large kitchen, searching for a sign that would give away the disaster that had occurred. Fortunately, I had already managed to dispose of much of the enormous puddle that had gathered around the oil can.

'Roger? She said. What's happened here?'

Roger had just finished wiping away most of the mess that had fallen onto the worktops and appeared to simply be carrying out the daily cleanup operation.

'Just cleaning up, Mrs Warner.' Said Roger, his chubby face all innocence.

She frowned at me before walking around the counter and surveying the floor.

'What's this mess? She said, looking down at a puddle of oil as a large drop landed on my head.

Rubbing my head I said: 'Oh, sorry, I er knocked into the oil can when I was cleaning the fryer, but at least that's nice and clean now.'

She looked at the fryer, which was rather ironically, sparkling clean.

'Tut, well just be careful will you! And instead of cleaning the blinking ceiling how about you start cleaning up this mess!'

'Ok, sorry about that.' I said as she began to walk off. Then, just as I was about to sigh with relief she turned back and looked at my clothes. I had forgotten that I was covered from head to foot in soup, gravy, carrot, oily water and bits of mop.

'And do you think you could wash your chef whites once in a while!' she barked 'what are the customers going to think if they see one of the chef's walking around in that state?'

'Ok, sorry.' I said.

'Well don't say sorry, just make sure you tidy yourself up before going downstairs!'

'Ok.' I said, getting close to the end of my tether and seriously considering throwing the oil can at her.

Sighing once more, she turned on her heels and walked away.

When I was sure she had gone, I looked up at Roger and he simply shook his head.

'Phew, that was close.' I said quietly and continued cleaning the ceiling.

On finally getting everything ship shape I managed to get to the end of my shift without any further catastrophes. As Roger went upstairs to get changed I made sure everything was switched off and made my way to the bathroom to try and make myself look a bit more presentable before going downstairs. Fortunately I had a spare, almost clean T shirt with me in the changing room, so I peeled the sodden one off and replaced it with the fresh one. Looking in the mirror I washed my face with hot water and surveyed the damage. Bloodshot eyes peered back at me from dark pits. I really needed to get a good night's sleep.

Making my way downstairs, Mrs Warner eyed me carefully from behind the self service counter to check that my appearance was acceptable, and, though I wouldn't win any awards for cleanest chef, at least I was no longer covered in gunge.

I made my way down to the cellar and clocked out, glad that I could finally get out of the place. Walking back upstairs I waved cheerfully at Mr Grimes and said 'See you tomorrow.'

Another day another dollar.

- Bob's Reading -

I had a shower and changed into my civvie clothes, glad to be clean. All I wanted to do was lie down and watch a bit of TV when my mobile rang. It was Bob.

Not tonight I thought, so I let the phone ring, and ring, and ring.

It must have rang fifty times – Bob's tenacity bordering on obsession.

Then I worried that something was wrong so I decided to pick up.

'Hello?' I said.

'Alright Hemsy.' Bob said. Nothing appeared to be wrong.

'Alright Bob, how's it going?'

'Not bad, how are you?'

'Not bad, you alright?' it sometimes went on like this for a while.

'Yeah, what's up?'

'I'm in town mate, just approaching your gaff now.'

Great, I thought. 'Alright I'll be right down. See you in a minute. Bye'

'Alright, bye.'

Two minutes later and Bob was standing at the front door.

'Alright Hemsy.'

'Hey Bob, how you doing?' I said.

'Alright mate, listen I want to talk to you about something. Do you want to come over to my place?'

'To be honest mate, I've had a really bad day today and...'

'Ay! Come on Hemsy! Bet you've just been languishing around your pit all day init. Have you just got up?'

'No!' I said 'I've been working – had a mental day I near...' he cut me up.

'Come on Hemsy, get your shit together, I've got stuff to do.'

I really should have told him to take a hike but the old gypsy lady was right, I *was* weak.

'Alright' I said.

The day was white once again and as we drove along the narrow causeway that connects Weymouth to the *Isle and Royal Manor of Portland*, I noticed that a thick fog was clinging to the island. It tended to be foggy quite a lot on Portland for some reason. It was like passing through a white veil to another world that hadn't quite caught up yet. Everything seemed to move very slowly when it was like this, like a dream. Ironically at that precise moment I noticed Teresa jogging along the causeway road towards Weymouth. As we passed, I waved out to her, but she didn't notice me.

'So how long did you stay at Flint's last night then, Hemsy, sorry for not taking you with us but you seemed a bit mashed. Didn't think we'd be able to move you!'

'Oh mate, it was a nightmare.' I said, having a flashback of the giant worm being ripped from my body.

'Yeah? How come?'

I snapped back to reality. 'Well, I'd already had a bottle of wine before we got there so all those bongs and pipes just did me in! I could barely move man!'

'Ha ha, Hemsy you *lightweight*!'

'That's not the worst though, I think I'm probably lucky to be alive!' I said, only half exaggerating.

'Yeah, how come?' he said smiling, as if relishing this bit of news.

'Well, like I say, I had far too much to drink and smoke and the combination sent me a bit, well *weird*.'

'Oh shit, you didn't start spouting bullshit to Flint did you Hemsy?'

'Not exactly. We were watching this horror film and I was like totally in my own head, unable to open my eyes, but I could hear these horrible noises of people being ripped apart and shit and it kind of got inside my head.'

'Is that all? Thought you were going to say something really bad happened.'

'Well, it did – because I was so fucked I started totally tripping and had a kind of waking nightmare of this enormous worm being ripped out of my body!'

'Urrgggh! You ain't right Hems! Ha ha!'

' That's not the worst of it though...all freaked out and shit, I puked all over Flint's carpet!'

Bob looked at me, open mouthed. 'No!'

'Yeah, it was nasty too, the crazy thing was, you know I said I was dreaming about this worm living inside me?

"Yeah..."

"Well I puked up what appeared to be sections of tapeworm man, it was *horrible*.'

Bob considered this for a moment. 'So you're telling me you puked up loads of skanky tapeworm shit onto Flint's carpet on the same night that he had a massive shipment of weed stolen and he *didn't* fucking *pulverise* you?'

'Well, Goodman was trying to goad him into giving me a kick-in but luckily he was so fascinated by the tapeworms that he didn't do anything.'

'You lucky bastard! That's mental oriental that is Hems. Ha ha, lucky son of a bitch!'

'I know! I'm pretty freaked out by the whole tapeworm business though.'

'That is pretty freaky, explains a lot though, I mean you eat like a fuckin horse man and you've always been a lanky streak of piss.'

'I know but it's horrible man! To think that some creature has been sharing my body, living off me like a parasite. The really weird thing is that ever since I first learnt about tapeworms back at school I've been really freaked out that one of those things could live inside you, it's just terrifying!'

'Yeah it is pretty skanky – ha hA!' Bob glanced over at me. 'Nah, seriously Hems, I bet it was just Flint fucking with you.'

'Yeah, I thought that too but how could he possibly know what my nightmare was about? It's like I made it happen. Also, I *saw* that shit in my puke man!'

I want to make ideas into reality, I thought and must have visibly trembled.

'Ah, don't worry about it man, I'm sure it's just a coincidence.'

Reaching the house, Bob killed the engine and we made our way inside.

'Hi, Jill.' I said, waving to Bob's mom, who appeared to be cooking dinner.

'Hello, Mark. How are you?' she asked.

'Not bad thanks, you ok?'

'Oh, can't complain!' she said with a good natured laugh.

I turned back to Bob and he was looking at me funny.

'Since when did you start calling my Mom, *Jill*?'

'What do you mean, that's her name isn't it?'

'Yeah, just don't start getting any ideas alright!' he said stomping up the stairs.

'Eh?' I said incredulously, following him.

He slid the sliding door open to his shoebox of a bedroom. Seriously, this was the smallest room you could possibly fit a bed in – there was just enough room for a small chest of drawers, a stereo and a small wardrobe, and all of it was really *squeezed* in so it felt a little bit claustrophobic.

Bob sat on the bed and turned his stereo on. A moment later and the Prodigy's *Music for the jilted generation* started to play. We all loved the Prodigy, but Bob in particular, he even had a poster of the band stood on one side of a chasm, giving the finger to a bunch of police who were crossing a rope bridge that one band member was clearly about to sever with a large knife. Underneath this painted scene sat the words, 'Fuck 'em and their law' - which was a line from one of their songs. This poster summed up Bob's attitude to the Police perfectly, he *hated* them. Mainly because he loved pot so much - quite possibly more than anything else in the world.

'What's that big bulge in your pocket Hems, you better *not* be *that* pleased to see me!'

'Oh, I forgot about those.' I said, opening the pocket on my combats and retrieving the Tarot pack that Terry had given me the day before. 'Terry roped me into being his look out again yesterday and I ended up with these as payment.'

'Nice.' Said Bob. 'Give us a reading then, Hems.'

'Well, it's been a while...'

'Ai, Ai! Come on now, Hemsy!'

'Alright alright. Let's take a look at these.' I said, opening the packet and pulling out a cardboard sleeve containing the deck and a reasonable sized booklet. 'Ok, I'm just going to do the major arcana because I don't really know the other cards.'

'Whatever you say Septic Peg, just get a move on.'

'Hey, you gotta respect the cards man, otherwise they won't work, you're supposed to wrap them in silk, and I always like to burn josticks when I do a reading. Do you have any?'

'I've got something better than that', said Bob, picking up a can of Orange zest air freshener and spraying it around the room. A wet mist hung in the air and burnt my eyes and lungs.

'Not quite what I had in mind!' I said coughing as Bob reached under the bed to reclaim a shoebox containing his smoking apparatus.

'Ha ha, got ya Hemsy!'

'Hmmm', I said, putting the deck aside for a moment and rolling myself a cigarette.'

'Ai! Ai! Oh I don't know about that Hems! I don't know about having those cancer sticks in here!' Bob said, a look of reproach on his face.

'Ok,' I said, preparing to put my tobacco away respectfully.

Bob looked at me and contemplated the decision before saying, 'Oh, alright then, you can smoke one.'

'Thanks.'

'I spose we *are* gonna need some josticks then in that case' he said, opening a drawer and pulling out some cannabis flavoured josticks, which I always found amusing because most people bought josticks to cover up the smell of cannabis.

'Oh cool.' I said, finishing the job of rolling the cigarette and lighting it.

Bob had finished re-assembling his bong and was burning his newly obtained 'soap-bar' into the bowl.

'Where did you get the hash from?' I asked.

'Spider.' He said.

'What? Is he still at Flint's house? I don't think he was there when I left.'

'Nah, he gave me his number last night and I went and met him down the back of the train station.'

'Do you reckon he *did* have Flint's gear away?'

'Don't know, don't care. Just needed a smoke mate, Spider supplied it, case closed.'

I thought back to the night before and remembered the characters from *Eastenders* talking about how Spider was going from one drug dealer to the next, ripping them off and making a fortune in the process. I turned to ask Bob what he thought about this but he was taking a big toke on his bong. When he finished, he offered it to me, but I refused, indicating the cigarette in my hand.

Blowing out a big plume of smoke that filled the room, Bob said, 'Come on then Hemsy, let's get these Tarot cards on the go!'

'Ok...' I said. Picking up the deck I held them face up and began sifting through them. Checking that they were in order, I counted the first twenty one, laid them out on the bed and placed the remaining cards back in the box. Then I took out the first card, *The Fool* and handed it to Bob face down.

'Ok, this card represents you...'

'Are you taking the piss?'

'No!' I said laughing nervously, 'seriously this is just what you're supposed to do, the fool always represents the person having the reading - it shows an innocent person on their journey through life, when you put it into the pack, it's supposed to represent your free will in the course of events, as represented by the other cards, or something.'

'Hmmm, alright. What have I got to do with it?' he said gesturing towards the card.

'Ok', I said, turning the rest of the cards face down. 'Just put the card in the deck anywhere you want.'

Bob looked carefully at the cards before putting the card at the top of the deck. Then, hesitating, he quickly took the card back and pushed it into the centre.

'Ok', I said, 'now, take the cards and give them a good shuffle, and, while you're doing that, try to think about any questions that you'd like to have answered.'

'Alright.' Bob said, taking the cards from me. Instead of shuffling them however, he dropped them face down onto the bed and proceeded to mix them all up. It was as if he thought this was a magic trick or something, and there was no way I was going to pull the wool over *his* eyes.

When he was satisfied, he collected the cards back into a neat deck and handed them to me.

'Right' I said, let's see if I can remember how this goes...' Keeping the cards face down, I placed the top card on the centre of the bed and placed the second card on top of this. Then I took the third card and placed it to the left of the first, the fourth card to the right of the first, the fifth card above the first and the sixth card below it. This made the sign of a Celtic cross. I always remembered the order of the layout because it was how I imagined a vicar gesturing the sign of the cross on his chest.

Down then across.

Next, the seventh card went to the bottom right of the cross and the remaining three cards lined up above this. This was the only proper layout I remembered, but Bob seemed suitably impressed and had taken on a quiet air.

Perhaps realizing that the Prodigy wasn't conducive to connecting with the primal energies of the universe, Bob swapped *Jilted Generation* for some *Enigma*, which I was surprised he owned. I raised an eyebrow at his selection and resumed the task.

'Ok, this first card is going to represent you as you are at the moment - your attitude and perception towards life and your general feelings about things.' I turned over the card to reveal *The Emperor*.

'Ha hA!' He laughed.

'Yep, well that's certainly about right!' I laughed.

'What does that mean then?'

'Well it's pretty much what you can see, the Emperor is a figure of great authority, strong willed and determined, who will stop at nothing to get what he wants, won't let anything stand in his way.'

'Yep, that's me.'

'Yep, that bloke at Flints house yesterday tried to stand in your way didn't he. Thought you were gonna knock him sparko.'

'I was! Ha hA!'

'Anyway, this card here' I said, picking up the card that lay on top of the Emperor, 'is your obstacle – something that *is* standing in your way.' I turned the card over and revealed it to be *The Fool*.

Looking at the card carefully, Bob said, 'That's Terry'.

'Eh?' I asked, presuming he was talking metaphorically.

He picked up the card and bought it closer to my eyes, 'Look at it man, that's actually Terry's face!'

I looked closely at the card and a chill went up my spine. Bob was right, the likeness was unmistakable. In the centre of the card, staring out at us, was the face of Terry, the fool.

'That's freaky man, you're right. You know, the Tarot is all about synchronicity and I think we have to assume that this card *does* actually represent Terry because we both had such a strong reaction to it.'

'Weird shit.' Said Bob, looking a little freaked out and toking on his bong. Blowing out another thick plume, he said, 'So what do you think that means?'

'Well, in this position it would usually indicate that you have to avoid making impulsive decisions, you have to tread carefully. But I'm thinking now that Terry might try to persuade you to make a bad decision or something.'

I looked from the card to Bob and he was sat stock still, staring at me.

'Mark, you don't realize how fucked up it is that you should say that.' He said, face deadpan.

'Why?'

'Alright, Hems, first of all you've gotta promise me that you won't tell *anybody* what I'm about to tell you. No-one ok?'

'Of course.' I said, now quite captivated.

Well, you know I said that I met up with Spider earlier to get some weed?'

'Yeah.'

'Well, he offered to hook me up with his contacts, said that the filth were all over them and that they needed to shift a shed load of weed *fast*. He asked me if I'd be interested in buying it for a *really* good price, said I could make a fortune off it.'

'Shit, what did you say?'

'Said I'd think about it. But he said I didn't have long as he was going to sell it on to the first lucky punter able to cough up the readies.'

'Do you have the er, readies?' I said.

'Well he wanted ten grand, which I *don't* have, but I *have* managed to put away about seven and a half, so I asked if he could do something for that. He said he would think about it as long as no-one came along with the full price first.'

'Jesus. Just how much weed are we talking about here?'

'I mean it Hems, not a word!' he paused, 'five kilos'.

'Five fucking kilos?! What are you even going to do with that much weed?'

'Shhhh, keep your voice down!' he smiled, 'I don't know, I was thinking about making myself a house out of it, like the marzipan house in Hansel and Gretel, only with no witch and instead of a giant furnace, there would be a giant bong, ha HA!'

'Seriously, Bob', I said, 'that's some heavy shit, you get caught with that and that's some serious jail time.'

'Don't you think I know that? Anyway, I haven't decided *what* I'm going to do yet.'

I looked at the cards and something occurred to me. 'Bob, was Terry there with you when you got the weed earlier?'

'Yeah.'

'And what did he say about the whole thing?'

'He said that he wished he had that much money because *he* would jump at the chance. Said that I would be a fool not to take the opportunity. I wasn't actually taking it that seriously until then but he persuaded me that I could make a fortune off it.'

I looked towards the obstacle card on the bed and Terry's eyes looked back at me.

'Well, it's difficult to say but I would suggest that this card might be telling you not to do this deal.'

'Oh, don't say that, Hems! Fuck sake it's just a coincidence that that looks like Terry's face. Let me see that book.' He said, snaring the Tarot book from where it sat on the bed. Flicking through the pages, he stopped at the one that indicated the meaning of the fool and read out the passage.

'Right, here it is' he said and began reading aloud. 'The fool represents the querant – innocent and pure, yada yada yada...ah, in contrast, it can also reflect the attitudes of others toward the querant, *their* belief that his or her actions have not been carefully considered.' There you go Hems, that could be talking about you.'

'Well, sure, I guess. Can I take a look', I said.

Bob handed me the book. Quickly skimming the lines he had just read, I read on.

'Hold on, this is what I was getting at, 'When the Fool card is revealed in this position in a reading, the querant should avoid impulsiveness, lest it lead to disaster.'

'Ok, Hems, I'll make sure I think things through carefully. Come on, what's next.' He said, lighting his bong again.

'Ok, this card represents the best outcome that you should aim for' I said turning over the card above the fool, *The Hanged Man*.

Bob exhaled another plume of dense smoke and peered through it at the newly revealed card. 'That's a bit depressing isn't it?' He coughed before continuing. ' The best thing I can do is to *hang* myself? Fuckin' hell! Ha HA!'

'No, it doesn't mean that. Obviously. I think it means that the best outcome is for you to do *nothing* and stay where you are. That's what the hanged man is all about - somebody staying still and not moving forwards.

'Hmmm, ok. Next?'

'Ok, this card represents your distant past', I said turning over the card to the left of the fool revealing it to be *The Hierophant*.

'Ok, hmmm that's interesting. I think this card represents your father.' Bobs Dad had been a staunch catholic who had turned his back on God and found Vodka instead, which ultimately made him turn his back on his family as well, leaving Bob to become the man of the house when he was just nine years old. I had never met him but I got the impression that he had left a dark smear on Bob's character, which might also explain why Bob had such an aversion to authority figures.

'What about my father?' Bob said, defensively.

'Well, he was quite religious, right?'

'Yeah.'

'Well the hierophant is like the pope, but it also stands for the leader of any religious order or dogma. It could also signify, therefore, a figure in your distant past who was an authority figure.'

'Interesting. What does that mean then?'

'Well, dunno, maybe the other cards will make it clearer.' I said, turning over the card below the fool and revealing it to be *Fortune*.

'Ok, this card represents your recent past, it shows that basically you've been going through the motions, having your share of good luck and bad luck, but I don't think it represents anything significant.'

'Ok.'

'Right, onto your future', I said turning over *The Tower*. I didn't like this card. It showed a tower that had been hit by lightning, red fire leaping out of the windows with two figures hurtling to their deaths. Not exactly positive imagery.

'Great.' Bob said, 'that looks nice. What does *that* mean?'

'Ok, it's perhaps not as bad as it appears, it usually signifies upheaval due to the hand of fate in your life, so could signify simply that a change is about to occur. It...' looking at the card, something strange caught my attention. In my old deck of Tarot cards, a man and a woman were depicted leaping to their deaths, but in this one it appeared to be two men. The face of one was angled away and could not be seen, but the other bore a marked resemblance to Bob. A shiver once again went up my spine and into my temples.

'What is it Hems?' Bob said, concerned at what I might have *seen* in the cards.

'Oh, nothing', I said, 'I was just thinking about what this might mean. To be honest I think it means that if you accept this deal it will be a big mistake and could create massive upheaval in your life.

'Ok, fair enough.' He said, 'what's next?'

'No seriously, Bob, this is a pretty freaky card and I think you should definitely *not* do this deal.'

'Al*right*!'

I moved on. 'Ok, this next card represents your best course of action,' I turned over *The Chariot*.

'Ha ha, no way!' I said.

'What?'

'Well, the chariot indicates that you have two choices, indicated by the black and white sphinxes there, but the reason that I'm laughing is that, the chariot is *my* card!'

'What do you mean, *your* card.'

'See that 69 symbol there? That represents *cancer*, that's my zodiac sign. So I think as this card is supposed to be your best course of action, you should listen to me and not do the deal.'

'That's not even fucking funny, Hems!' he said, jabbing me suddenly in the arm.

'Alright, alright, sorry.' I said, wanting to belabour the point but thinking it unwise. 'Alright, next we have your external factors' I said, turning over the *Death* card.

'Oh great!' said Bob.

'Don't worry this doesn't necessarily mean you're going to die.'

'Oh, *'not necessarily'* thanks a lot Hems!'

'No seriously, it usually means that there's a change about to happen, could be something really cool, pastures new and all that.'

'So it could be that I do this deal and things turn out rosy?'

'Or it could be that you do this deal and end up in the nick!' I replied.

'Shut up man! Alright, what's next?'

'Ok, next we have your hopes and fears' I said, revealing *the star*. This is a nice card actually, shows that you are very optimistic about the future and really want to make a success of things.'

'Yep, spot on.' he agreed.

'Ok, onto the final outcome' I said, turning over the final card, *The Devil*.

Bob had been in the middle of taking another toke on his bong and now coughed and spluttered at the sight of the card. Again, not a nice image. The card showed two naked figures chained to a beast with large horns brandishing fire.

'Wonderful stuff, well, thanks for coming, Mark, I must say I feel incredibly optimistic about the future now.' Bob said, putting on the voice of a TV presenter.

'Hey, it's not as bad as it looks', I said, thinking *this is the worst tarot reading ever*. 'The Devil simply means bondage...'

'Ooer missus!'

'Not that sort of bondage! Well, sometimes...but no it's usually about being tied to the material world in some way. Here, let's see what the book says.' I looked at the number on the card, fifteen, and turned to the appropriate page.

'Right, here we are, it says 'The Devil card indicates that the querant needs to be extremely cautious in the future to avoid becoming ensnared by the trappings of the world. If seen in the final position, this card often has dual meanings: on the one hand it indicates that the querant may be the victim of their own greed, entrapped by avarice; on the other an individual or individuals may be manipulating the querant for their own ends. Unless the querant steps back and assesses the situation carefully, they may soon find themselves irretrievably imprisoned.'

Whilst I read this, Bob had stopped smoking his bong and listened intently. We now sat in silence for a moment whilst he processed the reading.

He looked at me thoughtfully and then said, 'What a load of bollocks!'

- Past, Present and Future -

'Ok, Hems', he said, 'it's you turn!' He collected up the cards and returned them to the deck of the major arcana. 'That took a while though, could we just do a quick one?'

'Well, we could do a quick three card, past, present, future one for me.'

'Sound's good.' He said, handing me the cards.

'Ok.' I said, taking the cards and beginning to shuffle them. While I did this, Bob made yet another bong.

'Right here we go then, three cards - one, two, three. For the *past* I have...' I turned over the first card, *Strength*. The card depicted a lioness praying in the centre of a circle with lightning bolts shooting from her hands.

I want to be as strong as a lion, I thought, and had a flashback of my dream.

'This is freaky' I said, 'because, just last night I had a dream that I turned into a lion and defeated this demon creature , er, *thing*.'

'No way.' Bob said, possibly not too intrigued.

I thought about also telling him about the old gypsy and the three wishes but thought he would just make fun of me for getting conned out of six quid.

'Anyway, onto the present.' I said, turning over the second card and revealing it to be *The magician*. This card depicted a magician with a Yin Yang symbol next to each of his hands. 'Hmm this is an interesting one, this is cool actually, usually this is the card of a very rational person like a doctor or psychologist so perhaps indicates that I am quite balanced at the moment.'

'Are you sure it doesn't just mean you're good at doing magic tricks?'

'Ha ha, I said, 'no, well it usually just indicates someone who is able to...' *make ideas into reality*! I thought with a start and once again had a flashback to the tapeworms from the previous evening. Had I really brought them into existence through my own fear?

'Alright, Hems?' Bob said.

'Yeah' I said, 'just thinking.'

'Right let's see what your future holds!' said Bob, turning over the third card and probably hoping to see something horrible to balance out the negative cards he had in his reading.

'The *Universe*?' he said. 'What does *that* mean?'

I looked at the card carefully, it showed a complex configuration of interconnected lines and circles organized into a cross. In the four corners were the words, *Assiah*, *Yetzirah*, *Briah* and *Atziluth*.

'I have actually never seen this one before so I'm not sure what it means.'

'Ok, let's have a look in the book' said Bob, rifling to the correct page. 'Right here we go, 'The Universe - Great One of the night of Time...'

A shiver went up my spine and I thought of that terrifying night in the Abyss and then my third wish, *I want to live forever...*

Bob continued. '...is represented as a tree of life for each of the four worlds, *Assiah, Briah, Atziluth and Yetzirah* all interconnected via a central sephiroth, *Kether*, from which all life in the Universe emanates. This card indicates the omnipresent, omniscient and eternal nature of existence and presents an individual with the capacity to achieve enlightenment through the application of true will.'

Bob finished reading and closed the book. Well look at you with your fancy ass *Great one of the night of time* shit and all I get is flipping burning towers, death and the devil!

'You got the chariot too.'

'Yeah, thanks for that Hemsy. Forgot about that. Feel much better now! Ha hA'

It was getting late when Bob offered to give me a lift back into town. I almost refused; I didn't entirely trust Bob's driving when he'd had a few bongs - he was too confident and drove too *fast*. On the other hand, I really didn't want to have to wait at the bus stop for half an hour in the cold and I also didn't want to tell Bob that he drove like a madman - he didn't tend to take things like that very well.

So we drove.

The bit that really scared me was going around the top of *Old road*. It snaked its way down to the bottom of Portland at an incredibly steep gradient and at the top was a hair pin bend with a straight vertical drop over the side of a three hundred foot cliff. As we approached the bend, a vivid recurring nightmare was brought to mind. In it, I was on a bus in thick fog going around this very bend as we veered off the edge and plummeted into oblivion.

Bob clearly didn't share my fear of the cliff, seeming to accelerate as we approached the bend. My heart jumped into my mouth and I had to prevent myself from grabbing his arm as he swerved around the bend. The tyres screeched, but we stayed on the road. I looked to my left at the bright lights of Weymouth which pierced the darkness and painted the sea hundreds of feet below.

As my heart continued to race, Bob sped on, seemingly attempting to match its rhythm with the speed of the car, as if he were merely playing a video game where the only consequence of death was having to restart the race. We approached a second, only slightly less perilous bend to the left and once again, Bob applied his brakes a little too late, skidding the car around the corner - and into the blinding headlights of an oncoming car. There was a cacophony of screeching tires, a loud blast from the horn of the oncoming vehicle and a tangible *swoosh* as the two vehicles narrowly passed by one another.

Bob hammered *his* horn aggressively. 'Fuck off! Muppet!' he roared, his face red.

'Phew that was close.' I said.

'Yeah, nobhead!' Bob shouted again.

Perhaps the near collision scared Bob a little because he reduced his speed. Looking down, I realized that I was gripping the front of the seat and my body was tensed rigid.

'Alright, Hems?'

'Yeah.' I croaked. But I wasn't. I couldn't shake the image of *The Tower* tarot card and the two men that hurtled to their doom in Bob's future.

- Sign of the Time -

Upon finally returning to the sanctity of my home, I now lay in bed under the glow of a single yellow lamp and considered the events of the previous few days. First of all my mind turned to the oil explosion and how I had somehow managed to escape entirely unharmed. It reminded me of that scene from *Pulp Fiction* where, Samuel L. Jackson and, John Travolta were peppered with a magazine load of bullets that seemed to go straight through them to the wall beyond. That was pretty close to what I had experienced with the oil barrel, except of course I wasn't a gangster and instead of bullets peppering the wall, it was hot oil.

I want to live forever

Had the wish come true? Was I now invincible?

I picked up a cigarette lighter and deciding to test the theory by burning my hand.

'Yow!' I winced. Nope, not invincible. I mean, obviously. That was ridiculous. I had simply been far enough away from the oil can to not get hit. Perhaps the oil spattered on the wall behind me could have been caused by the oil rebounding from the ceiling and going straight over my head.

I remembered the incredulous expression on Roger's face as he assessed my position between the oil can and the oil spattered wall. It was true that I stood directly in the line of fire and did seem pretty miraculous that I hadn't got a drop on me.

It was a mystery. *I want to live forever* I thought again and wondered where I had conjured such a strange selection of wishes from in the first place. Probably most people would wish to win the lottery, or for world peace or something. Not me. I think that despite the fact that the gypsy had shocked me with knowing certain truths about me, I had ultimately still not believed that she had the power to grant wishes - I mean that was pure fantasy, wasn't it? I think that's why I wished for such abstract things; to test the woman - to prove that it could not be possible.

Then I thought about the tapeworm. Was it possible that I had conjured that into existence from my nightmare? Was this another reflection of the wishes come true? Had I now the ability to make ideas into reality?

No - if that were true I would surely be lying next to a beautiful blonde. An image of Teresa came into my mind.

I *had* been lying next to a beautiful blond before she had turned into that *creature*. But of course that was just another dream. I didn't even want to think about the lion I had turned into. Obviously this was merely *literal* wish fulfilment, again probably pieced together by my sub conscious.

But still, all of this nagged at my otherwise rational mind. I had always tried to keep an open mind but lately had succumbed more and more to science with its uncompromising necessity to demand proof. Having said this, I remained fascinated by the occult - Magic, Astrology, Palmistry and the Tarot. These ancient systems, if true, might reveal a deeper world at work, one with perhaps more meaning than the stark, cold existence presented by science. And if such a world of meaning *could* exist, perhaps that would lend more validity to the existence of God. For if there were a purpose to our lives, then maybe there was a creator of that purpose.

I was getting philosophical again and probably wouldn't sleep very well tonight. I looked at the alarm clock and saw that it was already twelve thirty but began to ponder the question of God once more.

Ever since I had grown old enough to question the validity of organized religion, I had been an agnostic. For me there was just too much evidence to suggest that most religions were organized for the sole purpose of power and control - an effective means of controlling the people. Catholicism, for example, has at its foundation the notion that you will go to hell if you don't act in accordance with Gods moral *laws*. What better form of manipulation than to leverage people's fear of death and what may lie beyond?

But, however corrupted many of the world's religions appeared to be to me, I still believed that there might be the possibility of a God that was not confined to the wrought attributes ascribed by the various faiths. For me there was still the possibility that God might represent an architect of sorts - a demiurge of the Universe, or maybe even the Universe itself. It all just seemed too complex to exist without the hand of creative agency.

Of course, atheists such as Richard Dawkins had a million counter arguments claiming that design is un-necessary, but I still didn't want to reject the notion out of hand. There was simply no evidence either way. For me though, life was beautiful and intricate and highly improbable, yet there to be a part of, to experience from land, air, sea and even space. With so much wonder to behold, it was hard for me to believe that it was mere chance, an accident of the ever weaving cosmos.

But if there was a God, then maybe He could hear me.

'If there truly is a God, give me a sign!' I whispered into the empty room.

I waited and listened, attempting to clear my mind of the myriad thoughts and images so that I might recognize a sign if one were to present itself.

I could hear the slow lapping of the sea outside my window and the soft humming of the wind. But no *signs* were revealed – not that I had really expected that.

Sighing, I turned off the bedside lamp, closed my eyes and drifted to sleep.

I awoke with a start, a dream lingering in my mind of burning towers and hooded figures.

Someone had whispered my name in the darkness.

I looked around and saw a tall figure standing at the door. Terrified, I sat up suddenly in bed, fumbling for the lamp switch on my bedside table. Almost knocking the lamp over, I managed to find the switch and immediately bathed the room in light. Nearly blinding myself, but holding my eyes open against the glare, I realized that the tall figure at my door had been nothing more than a collection of coats hanging there. *Phew!* I thought, relaxing a little. Wondering what time it was I looked around at the bedside table where my alarm clock sat and three digits shone back at me: 2:22. Strange, hadn't I awoken at this time last night? No, I remembered, I had awoken at this time in the *dream*! My eyes remained fixed on the three digits and an unexpected thought came into my mind: *Look at Time when tis short in the early hours.* Hadn't the gypsy woman said that? Was this what she had meant? Then I recalled the three two pound coins I had given her, one for each wish. Was this the sign I had asked for? If so, what did it all mean? I sat and stared at the red digits until a three and then a four consumed one of the two's. Unable to crack the enigma, I took one last look around the room before falling into a thankfully dreamless sleep.

The next day I awoke to glorious golden sunlight coursing through my curtains, the sound of seagulls and the smell of sea salt wafting through the open window. I looked at my alarm clock and saw that it was ten thirty. I was late for work – again! Then, leaping out of bed I paused - it was Wednesday – I had the day off.

There was no better feeling than thinking you had to work and then realizing that you had the whole day to do with as you pleased. With this thought, I opened the curtains wide, revealing a skinny man in his boxer shorts to a host of passersby. I received a shocked look from an old lady, followed by a slightly creepy smile and then decided to close the curtains again, at least until I was dressed.

After getting showered and dressed I made my way out the door to greet the world. It was a glorious day and the sun left a line of brilliance glistening across the surface of the sea where I was sure unknown adventures awaited. I breathed in deep lungfuls of fresh, sea air and walked with purpose into the town. Passing the *Crows Nest*, I waved at Mr Grimes, who was in the process of flipping an egg. He waved back at me mouthing, *Maximus*! I smiled and walked on quickly to avoid the evil clutches of the Duchess and the possibility that she might call me in to cover someone's shift. It certainly wouldn't be the first time. Because I lived next door to work, she had once called up to me whilst I was otherwise engaged in the sack. My then girlfriend had asked me if the Duchess was my mother and I simply replied that it was the *bloody Duchess* before continuing our love making to the far from dulcet tones of Mrs Warner 's insistent shouting.

Anyway, I needed to get that place out of my mind, because today was *my* day. I was going to do a bit of shopping, grab some lunch from *Picnics* - the best sandwich shop in the known Universe - and then maybe I'd go and see if there was anything decent on at the cinema. Passing *W. H. Smiths* I looked in and noticed that they had gotten a new security guard. I made a mental note to tell Terry that they were clearly tightening security and were probably on to him. Then I noticed a sign saying 222 in bold white lettering on red. *What the hell?* I thought, stopping dead, then I realized that it was actually three signs, each offering *3 for 2* but from my perspective the first part of each sign was obscured. 'Ha, just coincidence', I said to myself.

Trying to put the 2's and all of the weirdness that came with them out of my mind I headed towards my first stop for the day - the old surf shop by the harbour. You could usually get good deals on summer clothes there – not least because it was now nearly winter. I was just a poor chef – I couldn't afford *Armani* or *Benetton*, or even *Topman* for that matter - if I could find good brands for low prices then I was happy. Approaching the surf shack I noticed two racks outside with t-shirts advertised at £5. Bargain.

Walking over to the racks I started sifting through them. There were some good brands here in amongst the tat: *Quicksilver, Animal, Billabong*, to name but a few but most of them were a bit too garish; oranges that threatened to burn out your eyes if you looked directly at them and others that would have you immediately arrested by the fashion police. This probably explained why they were on the cheap racks. As I rifled through the assortment however, one t-shirt in particular caught my attention. It was a much more subdued colour than the rest, just a simple beige with a light blue design. On it were emblazoned three symbols, a star of David, a Celtic cross and a yin yang symbol. Above these were printed the words *Spirit of Harmony* in a Celtic looking font. Though it was a bit *New age* I knew immediately that I *had* to have this t-shirt - that it was perfect for me. In fact I had the strangest feeling that it had been *intended* for me, even though I knew that this was absurd.

Scooping the T-shirt and its hanger off the rack, I took it inside the shop. Inside it smelt of bamboo and sun tan lotion and there were surf boards flanking the till. On the racks inside the shop were colourful Hawaiian shirts, one or two of which I had purchased the year before.

'Hi there, can I help?' said a voice from my right. I turned to see a girl of maybe twenty two who appeared to be in the middle of restocking a display of designer sunglasses.

'Hey, yeah, just this please.' I said, holding up the t-shirt.

As the girl took it from me, she smiled. 'Would you like to keep the hanger?'

She had piercing green eyes, a ring through her nose, and dreadlocks. And she was cute. Also, I recognized her from somewhere but couldn't quite place her.

'Er, no, that's fine thanks – got too many already.'

'Hey, I know you,' she said, 'you're that guy who puked up on Flint's floor aren't you?'

Now I remembered, she was painted toes girl!

'Ah, erm...'I wanted to lie but realized it was futile 'yeah.'

'Sorry, I didn't mean to put it like that, that must have been quite embarrassing.'

'Yeah, a little.'

'I tell you what though mate, I'm amazed you made it out of there alive, especially the mood Flint was in.'

'Nah, I would have kicked his ass.' I said.

The girl gave me a curious look and then realized I was joking. 'Ha ha, no seriously, he can be one nasty piece of work.'

'Why do you go round there then? I mean, he wasn't exactly a gentleman towards you.' I said, remembering how he had flung her into the wall.

The girl seemed suddenly defensive. 'Well to be honest it's the only place round here I could get some good weed, everywhere else seems to have dried up.'

'Yeah I heard that. What about Spence, do you know him?'

'Yeah, Spence, Fudge, Scowse Steve...'

'Scowse Steve is dealing?' I laughed.

'Yeah, well I think he realized that it was a damn sight easier to carry around a couple of ounces of weed to a few bottles of Vody!'

'Ha ha, yeah, Steve's a funny bloke, I remember getting stoned with him one day and all he kept saying was things like...' I adopted a scowse accent *'Pink Floyd, dey were a good band...'*

And we both said in scowse accents: 'Weren't dey doh?'

Laughing, the girl said: 'Are you out later?'

I hadn't got any plans to be but wanted to look cool. 'Probably, yeah, what you up to?'

'Was thinking about going to *Larry's*, so maybe I'll see you there yeah?'

'Yeah, ok. I'll see you then.' I smiled and made my way to the door.

'Hey aren't you forgetting something?' she called out.

I turned back, thinking, absurdly, that she was asking me to give her a goodbye kiss - but then I realized that I had left the t-shirt behind. Embarrassed, I could feel my cheeks burning as I walked back to the counter and took hold of the bright blue bag. 'Doh! Thanks.' I said, walking away for the second time.

Leaving the store I had to squint my eyes for a moment against the glare of the sun. I chanced a quick backwards glance into the store and saw that the girl - damn I had forgotten to ask her name - had resumed her work stacking the display case. I hadn't noticed it before at Flint's place, but she was *fine* and I decided I would have to see if Bob and Terry wanted to go to *Larry's* later.

Feeling peckish, I let my stomach do the walking – down the backstreets near the harbour to the best bun shop in the world. There was always a small queue here, especially near lunch time, which was a testament to the awesome quality and value of the rolls. There was a great selection too, with Chinese chicken, Coronation chicken, Lamb and mint and Thai chicken, to name but a few of my favourites. As I waited I made up my mind that today was definitely a Chinese chicken day.

Making a hole in the brown paper bag through which to eat my delicious lunch, I walked back towards the beach so that I could eat with a view. On the way I passed the arcade on the beach. Coins *chinged*, and a mechanical monkey sang a verse from the jungle book: *You know it's tru-u-u, I wanna be like you-u-u.*

It was a beautiful day, and though it was October, the great weather and the lapping of the waves on the beach made me feel like I was on holiday.

I sat and watched the waves for a while, enjoying my lunch and trying to decide what to do with the rest of the day. Looking at my watch I almost choked as I saw that it was twenty two minutes past two. I took a moment to contemplate this before once again putting it down to coincidence.

Finishing my lunch I tossed the brown paper bag into the nearest rubbish bin and decided to head to the cinema and see if there was anything worth watching.

Ten minutes later I was standing in the foyer looking at a pamphlet advertising film times and one particular film caught my attention: A film simply entitled, 'Pi'. Its summary read:

A paranoid mathematician searches for a key number that will unlock the universal patterns found in nature.

Huh. Universal patterns found in nature. I wondered if that was what I was seeing. Could the two's be some sort of emergent pattern. I had to watch this film!

After purchasing a ticket, a coke and a large bag of minstrels I made my way to screen two - had to be - which I was happy to discover was completely empty.

This would be my own private showing and I could pretend that I was a millionaire with enough money to afford my own cinema screen. Life was good.

Placing my coke in the hole in the arm rest I relaxed into the padded chair and looked up at the screen.

The adverts were still playing and five *Minis* raced around an Italian city in a parody of the Italian job. It was one of those *Mini adventure* adverts that seemed to get more and more ludicrous. In this one, the minis appeared to be battling flying saucers and as lasers threatened to obliterate the leading mini it sped forwards towards the cinema screen. To my absolute wonderment the mini's number plate read simply *222* and as the car sped forwards, this number was painted thirty feet high across the screen. The advert finished with the usual *It's a mini adventure* tagline and I just stared at the screen slack jawed. I looked around to see if anyone else had entered but I was still alone. My own personal screening had become a little spooky.

That did just happen didn't it? Surely this was going far beyond the realms of coincidence?

As I thought this the lights went down and the curtains drew apart to reveal the full width of the screen. The film began and captivated me from start to end. It was about a mathematician genius called Max who believed that there were universal patterns in nature that could be identified as numbers. Stock traders tried to manipulate Max's genius to get an advantage on the stock market and a Chasidic Torah scholar believed that the numbers were a message from God.

It was a very good film, which left me somewhat shaky and I was glad of, and slightly surprised by, the glaring sunlight that greeted me when I exited the cinema. Despite the sunlight, the day had gotten a bit cooler now and the day's business was slowly drawing to a close.

As I walked I decided I'd better check if anyone had called whilst I had been otherwise incommunicado. I fished my mobile out of my pocket and saw that Bob had called, so I gave him a call back. He answered almost immediately.

'Hello, Hemsy?'

'Hey Bob, what's up?'

'Mark! Shit man, you've got to come to Terry's, he's really fucked up man!'

'What do you mean? What's happened?'

'Can't explain right now, just get over here as soon as you can, ok?'

'Sure, ok – I'm on my way. See you soon.'

'Alright, see you in a minute.'

Perplexed, I put my phone in my pocket and started jogging. I didn't have a clue what had happened but it sounded serious. Passing the beach I had a bit of a start as I noticed the old gypsy sitting alone in one of the bus shelters. I wondered if she had any idea the trouble she had caused me over the last few days. She didn't appear to, and that's what was frightening about it. Never mind, didn't have time to think about that right now, from the way Bob spoke it sounded like something bad had happened so I began to run.

Approaching Terry's house I could see that the door was open. Not as unusual as you might think - Junkies and drunks had a tendency to forget simple things such as closing the door behind them. I let myself in and closed the door behind me, before shouting out: 'Terry?'

'Up here Mark,' said Bob, 'quick give me a hand, quick!'

I ran up the stairs and into Terry's bedsit. He was lying on the bed, his face lolled to one side, the remains of what looked like vomit, or possibly just drool, drying on his chin.

'What happened? Is he drunk?'

'Fuckin' junkies that's what happened!'

'What?'

'They gave him fucking methadone didn't they, on top of god knows how much he already had to drink today!'

'Shit!' I said, rushing over to the bed and peering into Terry's face. He was so still that for a terrifying moment I thought that he was dead before noticing the slow swelling of his chest.

'Hey, Terry, wake up!' I said, shaking him by the shoulder, 'Yo, Terry, it's Mark, man, wake up!'

Nothing.

'It's not doing any good. I've been trying to wake him up for ages, Mark, what are we gonna do?'

'I dunno,' I said, trying again one last time, 'Terry! Terry! Wake up!' This time I slapped him round the face, then realising that it had no effect, slapped him again – hard. This time there was a small murmur.

'That's it Hems! He just moved' Bob said, moving closer to take my place.

Looking down at him with concern I had an idea. 'Wait here,' I said before making my way hastily out of the room and down the stairs. As I descended, the staircase trembled and creaked uneasily as the rotten wood strained under my weight. Running into the kitchen, I located a relatively clean looking glass amongst the debris of leftovers and cigarette butts and filled it with cold water.

Arriving back into the room, I pushed past Bob and splashed a little water in Terry's face.

No reaction.

Looking at the glass I decided to empty its entire contents over Terry's head. This seemed to do the trick a little as he again murmured and opened his eyes a fraction.

'Right, we've gotta get him up,' Bob said. 'Give me a hand Mark.'

'Ok, you take one arm, I'll take the other,' I said and we started hoisting him up. But he was heavy, and was a complete dead weight so it was not easy.

'Ok, on three - one, two, threeyup.'

We lifted Terry into a half standing position and his head lolled to the side, but again, there was a murmur.

Staggering slightly, Bob lifted up Terry's face and shouted close to his ear 'Come on Terry, you gotta wake up man!'

Struggling with the weight, I looked at Bob's face and was surprised to see that tears were forming in his eyes.

'We've got to try and get him some fresh air,' I said. 'do you think we can get him down the stairs?'

'Well, we can try.'

'Alright come on man, use your legs, Terry! Oi Terry, stop being a lazy bastard and walk!'

Another murmur and Terry's legs did start to move by reflex as we walked him towards the door. Squeezing through the doorway I tried to make sure that Terry's lolling head didn't hit the door frame but as we came through, Bob caught his shoulder, releasing more splinters of wood to join the pile on the floor.

'You, alright, Bob?' I panted, struggling with the weight.

'Yeah. I'll live.'

Making it onto the landing, I once again worried that the floor wouldn't hold our weight as the floorboards creaked and even seemed to dip slightly, but held.

'Come on Terry', Bob said in Terry's ear, 'We're going down the stairs now and it's not easy so if you could help us out it would be much appreciated mate.'

We started moving down the stairs, brushing the side of the wall, half carrying, half dragging Terry between us in an awkward diagonal squeeze. Then, about four steps from the bottom, one of the rotten steps finally gave up the ghost as Bob and Terry stood on it together. Falling through to the next step, Bob instinctively let go of Terry who went flailing forwards, carrying me with him as we tumbled down the stairs like a couple of crash test dummies. Several bangs, crunches and yells of pain later and Terry and I lay on our backs at the bottom of the stairs.

'Aaaaoow! Motherfucker!' howled Bob in pain.

I looked up to see him sprawling halfway up the stairs, his right foot painfully lodged to the ankle in the broken step.

I winced, raising my head to see if anything was broken. I had bruised my arm pretty badly and braised my knees and shins on the stairs, but other than that, I was ok.

'You ok, Bob,' I asked as he yanked his foot out of the broken step and massaged his ankle.

'I think so.' He said, his face flushed red. 'Just done my ankle in a bit, but I'll live. How's Terry?'

Terry was lying on the floor to the side of me, slumped awkwardly on his shoulder. It looked like he had grazed at least one of his arms and probably his legs too, I checked to see if he was breathing and felt a faint but steady pulse.

'Terry!' I yelled, once again, smacking his cheeks. This time he uttered a faint murmur.

Bob joined us at the foot of the stairs. 'Come on then, let's get him outside.'

With our mutual injuries, it was even more difficult this time to lift Terry up and we almost fell into a heap as Bob teetered on his bad foot.

Awkwardly opening the door with my free hand, I managed to pull it aside and made my way into the daylight, trailing Terry and Bob behind me like a geriatric caterpillar ambling into the light. The air was refreshing after the stale air in the flat and I was thankful that it was also a little brisk. Perhaps this would help to wake Terry up - I really hoped so because I was starting to get really worried.

'Maybe we should have just called an ambulance,' I said as we hobbled out of the house.

'Maybe, though I think this might work, he keeps making little moaning noises.'

I listened for a moment as we walked and Terry did seem to be mumbling.

'Terry!' I shouted, 'you alright mate?'

'Mmmmm blarshes!'

'Jesus man, you're starting to sound like Wingnut now! I told you you ought to lay off the booze didn't I!'

'Boshta Hems'

'Come on Terry, you've got to walk man, we're outside, you've got to wake up and walk. Can you do that?'

'ummm whads, um why, wha?' he said, his eyes struggling to open.

'Good, good, come on Terry, we've got to run.' I said increasing the pace a little.

Terry lifted his head up a fraction and managed to partially open his right eye.

'Talk to me man! It's me, Bob, how you doin?'

'Bainburrry' slurred Terry. I was starting to get a bit concerned. What if the mixture of booze and methadone - not to mention the fall down the stairs - had inflicted serious brain damage? I remembered watching a documentary called *The Frozen Addicts* about a group of unfortunate junkies who had all injected a dodgy batch of heroine and had ended up with a form of Parkinson's where they became frozen in persistent vegetative states. Many of them stayed like that for the rest of their lives, completely unable to communicate with the world but remaining perfectly conscious and aware. A living hell in other words.

'Where?' Terry said, beginning to open his eyes more fully.

'Oh, thank Christ' I said.

'Just going for a bit of an afternoon stroll, Terry.'

'Wha? Where'd you come fro Bainbur...Bain..bury?'

'Out of the sky mate, now start moving your legs ya cunt!'

Terry began to walk more normally and slowly began to come around.

We had walked to the end of the street and as we turned to walk back in the opposite direction, some idiot in a car sped past us and shouted out. 'Wankers!'

Bob turned around immediately. 'Yeah, come back here and say that then you fucking prick!'

The car screeched to a halt and began reversing back towards us.

Oh no, this is all we need.

Bob began to slip out from beneath Terry's arm so that he could take on whoever was driving. Before he could do so, the car pulled up parallel with us and a cocky youth wearing a bright green cap gave us the finger before tossing something out of the car. The McDonalds milkshake hit Terry square in the face and the plastic cup fell apart, covering him in strawberry milkshake. Laughing hysterically the youth was too slow on the accelerator as Bob reached through the window and grabbed hold of his arms. The youth shrieked and the car bunny hopped forwards, but Bob held on.

'Not so fucking clever now are ya?' shouted Bob into the boys face.

The car bunny hopped forwards again and this time, Bob could no longer hold on. There was a tear as the youths t-shirt ripped and Bob half fell into the road as the car sped forwards. As it disappeared hurriedly into the distance the passengers in the back seat looked back at us with pale faces.

'Fucking prick!' shouted Terry.

Me and Bob turned around and looked at him, his face still dripping with ice cold milkshake, now completely awake.

'Come on lads, I need a drink,' he said.

'No you fucking don't Terry, you fucking twAt!' said Bob, walking over to Terry and shoving him hard into the wall of the house.

'Whoa, man chill out, what's wrong with you?'

'You're what's wrong with me you selfish cunt! Me and Hemsy have probably just saved your fucking stupid life, nearly killing ourselves in the process and all you want to do is go and have another fucking go at killing yourself. I've had enough of it.'

Terry frowned. 'Look, Bainbury, I didn't ask you to do nothing, right, just calm down and have some respect alright!'

'Respect. Jesus, you're such a wanker Terry do you know that? What's it gonna take for you to stop drinking, and what was it today, fucking *methadone*? What are you a fucking junky now?'

'What?'

'Yeah, your junky neighbour, Jed told me. Said you loved a bit of the methadone, told him it was the best thing you ever did, until of course, you nearly slipped into a coma!'

'I didn't nearly slip into a coma!'

'Oh yeah, ask Hemsy what it took to wake you up. We had to slap the shit out of you - Hemsy poured water over your head...'

'You poured water over my head? What the fuck, Hems?'

'You're fucking right I did, you prick!'

'What the fuck? Don't call me a fucking prick, Hems or we are really going to fall out.'

'Yeah whatever, I'm outa here.'

'Oh you think you can call me a prick and just walk away?' said Terry, giving me a sharp poke to the ribs.

On instinct, I turned around and punched him hard in the face, shattering his nose. The force pushed him against a window and one of the pains smashed, causing a man inside the house to shout out in alarm.

Terry put his hand to his nose, which was gushing with blood and looked at me, astonished.

'You deserved that, Terry,' said Bob.

'Fucking hell, what is wrong with you two? Give me a fucking break will ya!' he said, holding onto his nose and pushing himself up from the windowsill.

At that moment a middle aged man opened the door to the house and yelled in a thick Birmingham accent. 'What the bloody ell do you lot think you're doing? You're gonna flippin pay for that!'

Bob, Terry and I turned around to look at the man and shouted in unison. 'Fuck off!'

The man looked at Terry, covered in milkshake with blood running from his nose and then looked at our faces and quickly made his way back inside.

'I'm sorry I hit you man, but you've got to understand that you have put us through hell this afternoon. We thought you were gone man – if Bob hadn't gotten to you when he did, you probably would have been!'

'Really, you think it was that bad?'

'Well, Terry, ask yourself, how did you get outside?'

'Erm, well...'

'I'll tell you how you got outside, me and Hemsy had to pick you up off your bed, *fall* down the stairs with you, drag you into the streets and walk you about for twenty minutes. Ha, it took that little prick chucking milkshake in your face for you to actually wake up!'

'Shit, really?'

'Yeah, really. Look at my foot, man' Bob said, leaning against the wall to reveal bloodstained socks.

'Alright, sorry, Bob.' Terry said, wiping blood and milkshake on the disgruntled mans windowsill.

'Ok, I need to sit down,' said Terry, walking in the direction of his house. Bob and I followed, the three of us hobbling like old ladies.

We made our way into the house and closed the door just in time to see a police car racing around the corner and screeching to a halt at the house that we had just left.

'Fucking Pigs!' said Bob, watching the road through a crack in the curtains.

Terry went through to the bathroom, putting the kettle on as he did so.

'Make us a coffee, Hems' he said through the open door as he washed the muck off his face.

'Okay.' I said.

'That's quite a right hook you've got on you there, Hems. You were lucky you caught me off guard with that one.'

'Yeah, right.' I said smiling.

'It's a good job you had a good reason, otherwise things would be very different I tell ya.'

'Yeah, well he did have a good reason didn't he, Terry, nearly knocked you sparko! Ha hA, good for you, Hemsy!'

'Shut up, Bob.' Said Terry.

I made three coffees and handed one to Terry as he made his way back into the kitchen towelling his hair. He snatched the mug from my hand, glaring at me with one of his *mean* faces.

'Do either of you happen to have a paracetemol or anything, my head is fucking killing me!'

'I'm not surprised, looks like Hems has given you a black eye!'

'What?' said Terry, alarmed 'no he hasn't Bob, shut up man.' To make sure, he wiped condensation off the kitchen window in an attempt to use it as a mirror.

'Yep, think you're gonna need a nice raw steak for that one, Terry. Ha hA!'

Terry continued to assess the damage before turning to give me a dirty look.

Walking into the lounge and passing Bob his coffee, I was about to sit down when I heard a large bang and a *yelp*. Making our way into the hall we looked down on Wingnut, who lay face down halfway down the stairs - his foot still protruding from the now gaping hole in the stairs.

Wearing a ragged blue dressing gown and little else, he looked up and pointed at me.

'Farrrking Police!' he yelled, before letting his chin drop with a slap onto the step.

- Painting the Town Red -

I offered to help Wingnut up but he pulled his arm away, still convinced that I was one of the apparently maligned boys in blue.

'Alright.' I said, stepping back while Bob helped him to his feet. Wingnut had also sustained an injury to his ankle and he hobbled, with Bob's help to his bedsit, mumbling something incoherent as he passed.

Walking back into the lounge, I finally sat down with a sigh.

Terry appeared to be sobering up now and was starting to look half way back to normal. Rubbing at the minor scrapes he had sustained on the trip down the stairs earlier, he looked at Bob. 'So, have you spoken to Spider about that thing we discussed yet?'

'No. Haven't decided what I'm going to do yet.'

'What do you mean man? If you've got the money, you'd be crazy not to rip his arm off – you could make a fortune, not to mention having your own persy for a long time to come! What's the problem?'

'Nothing. Just don't want to make the wrong decision, that's all – it's a lot of weed – if I get caught with that I'm going to be saving up my bread in the nick init!'

Terry laughed mischievously.

'Saving up your bread?'

'Aw he's so sheltered isn't he! Not a clue!' said Terry.

'Ha ha,' laughed Bob, 'did you know that Jed had spent some time inside on some GBH charge?'

'No, but that doesn't surprise me' I said 'that guy looks like a psycho.'

'Yeah, well, apparently he did some bloke over with a spanner for looking at him funny.'

'Shit.'

'Anyway, he reckons that the *lifers*, you know the real *nasty* criminals who were in there for murder and shit – well apparently those guys used to save all of their bread up, you know that they'd get for their daily allowance and shit, they'd save it up for a special occasion.'

'Eh?'

Terry took over, barely containing his laughter. 'They'd save it up until they had about eight slices and then they'd squidge it all together so it was all doughy.

Apparently the consistency is as close as you can get to the proverbial toothless gibon!'

'Eh?' I said.

Bob laughed and shook his head 'he's talking about a girl's minge!'

'Aw, that's gross man!' I said disgusted.

'Nah,' Bob said, 'what's gross is, they would need to save up a good few slices over the course of a week in order to have enough, and in that time a lot of it would have gone all mouldy!'

'Urrgh!' I said, pulling a face.

'Come on though, Bob' said Terry suddenly serious 'you're not going to end up in the nick when you've got your homies covering your back, init?'

'Seriously Terry, what are we gonna be able to do against the police?' I said.

'Shut up Hems! Hey, you haven't been listening to old wussy Hemsy, have you Bob, cos this cowardly shit ain't like you.'

'Don't call me a fucking coward, Terry.'

'Look, all I'm saying is, this is a fucking sweet deal and it sounds to me like the only reason you're not taking it is cos your wussing out.'

'No, you look, Terry, this isn't like scoring an eighth or something, we're talking about five kilos! If I get caught with that, that's some serious time!'

'But, you're not going to get caught are you.'

'How can you be so sure the deal's kosher anyway?' I intervened. 'I mean, does it not strike you guys as a bit odd that after doing the deal with Spider, Flint's stash miraculously disappeared?'

'Bollocks, Hems,' said Terry, 'you know that weren't Spider man, he was busy dealing at Flint's when that gear went missing.'

'Yeah, well, that's hardly conclusive is it? I mean, he easily could have arranged for one of his *contacts up north* to break in and take the weed. He was probably one of the only people who knew where it was kept'

'He's got a point there.' Said Bob.

'I can't believe this shit. You know Spider, man! He's one of the soundest people we know! And I can't believe you, Hems! What would he think of you if he heard you talking about him like this? All two faced and shit.'

That made me feel a bit guilty because the truth was, I *did* like Spider and I didn't want to think that he was capable of doing the dirty on Bob, but there was no escaping the fact that it was all a bit dodgy.

'Well, I suppose you've got two options 'avent you Bainbury. Either you can wuss out and listen to Hems' shit, or you can step up to the plate, grow a set of kahunas and be a man about the whole thing.'

'Shut up, Terry – it's my fucking money, I'll make my own mind up.'

'Fairish nuff. Just remember you'd be a fool not to do this.'

Bob frowned at that. Maybe it was Terry's choice of words, *you'd be a fool.* Maybe he was thinking that of the two possible meanings of the fool tarot card one might be that he would be a fool if he *didn't* do the deal.

'Anyway,' I said, changing the subject, 'do you guys fancy going to *Larry's* later?'

'*Larry's*, on a Tuesday night?'

'Yeah, well, you know when we were at Flints the other night and he pushed that girl over?'

'Yeah, fucking nasty piece of work. What about it?' Said Bob.

‘Well I er met her in that surf shop by the harbour earlier and she asked me if I wanted to join her at Larry’s later.’

‘Are you fucking mental, Hems?’ said Terry.

‘Why?’ I said.

‘You know that’s Goodman’s bird don’t ya?’

‘Nah, I don’t reckon. I asked her why she goes round Flint’s and she said it was just for the weed.’

‘And Goodman's cock.’ Said Bob.

‘Nah, I don’t reckon. Anyway, there’s no harm in going along and having a look is there?’

‘Can’t believe this Hems, you’re there having a go at Bob for taking risks and shit and there’s you ready to get your nob wet on a dealers bird!’ said Terry.

‘God, I wish I hadn’t mentioned it now, look I’m going anyway so do you guys fancy coming along?’

‘Well we’re gonna have to go now just to look after your arse aren’t we?’ said Bob.

‘Hems!’ said Terry, once again giving me one of his exaggerated mean faces whilst wiping blood from his nose. I wasn’t sure if he was admonishing me for suggesting that we go out or for his bleeding nose.

'What time you going then, Hemsy?' said Bob.

I looked at my watch and saw that it was nearly seven thirty. 'Well I was thinking about nine-ish. Could do with some grub first though. I tell you what, if you guys come with me tonight, I'll treat you to a nice pizza, yeah?'

Terry's eyebrows lifted. '*Munchies*?' he said, referring to the towns best pizza place.

'Hell yeah, twelve inch.'

'That's what *she* said!' said Bob and we all laughed.

Taking orders of a pepperoni pizza for Bob and an Hawaiian for Terry I set off into the night for *Munchies*. Hopefully it shouldn't be too busy at this time – later on would be a different story though. *Munchies* was the place everyone went to for their late night food after the pubs and clubs kicked out. Virtually the whole town would be queued up in the street where many a fight would break out. I doubted the pensioner tourists who came here to eat in the *Crows Nest* would ever suspect that the town was such a jungle in the early hours of the morning.

Reaching *Munchies* I found it empty and so was able to order my food straight away. The guy behind the counter went to school with my older sister who apparently was something of a hit - all of the blokes in her year seemed to know her and somehow they all also seemed to know that she was my sister. This could be quite useful on occasion as I found myself getting freebies in exchange for *putting in a good word* with her.

'Hey Steve, how's it going?' I said approaching the counter, an intoxicating aroma of mushrooms and batter greeting me.

'Hey up mate' Steve said 'how's your sister?'

'Yeah, she's alright mate.'

'Well, what can I get you on this fine evening?'

'Can I have a twelve inch pepperoni, a twelve inch Hawaiian and a twelve inch mighty meaty please.'

'You sure can – I'll see if I can throw in a garlic bread for you as well, alright mate.' He said winking.

'Nice one mate – that would be sound!'

As I waited I watched the world outside as the town slowly came to life for the evening. Pubs were starting to fill and the sound of high heels hitting concrete filled the streets.

After a while, Steve returned with four large boxes.

'There ya go, matey!' He said, laying the boxes on the counter.

'Thanks, Steve, nice one mate!'

'No worries buddy,' he said giving me a wink, 'Hey tell your sister I said hello, yeah?'

'Will do mate.' I said, as I walked out.

So as not to let the pizzas cool I decided to take a shortcut down one of the alleyways that cut nicely through the streets. On my way I began to question my decision as the lights from the street retreated meaning I had to take it quite slowly in order to avoid falling over in the murk. About halfway down I noticed a hooded figure in the distance and my heart rate quickened as I had a bout of anxiety. Just keep walking. Head down. Ignore him, whoever he is.

As I came level with the hoodie, he lifted his head. 'Have you got a fag man?' His accent was thick Geordie and I only just understood what he said.

Thinking about it I decided I could do with one myself. 'I've got a fag if you've got a lighter.'

'Why ai man.' He replied stereotypically, fishing a lighter from his pockets.

In the limited light I could make out that he was a thick set broad shouldered man, mid twenties with dark eyes.

For some reason they seemed to make people bigger up north, and I suddenly felt a little uneasy.

In order to reach into my pocket and find my cigarettes I had to put the pizzas down for a moment. This was a good opportunity to get out of the alleyway. 'Hey, I'm just going to put these down over here.' I said putting the pizzas down on a step and reaching into my pocket for the cigarettes. Finding them, I fished out two, handing one to the hoodie and putting one into my mouth.

The hoodie lit my cigarette and in the flame light I noticed that he appeared to be grinding his jaw. 'So, you a student like?'

'No, I'm a chef man.'

'Where's that like?' he said, but before I had a chance to answer, he picked up my pizzas from the step and began to walk away from me.

'Whoa, what are you doing?' I said, pulling level with him and grabbing his arm.

The punch came out of nowhere, smashing into my jaw with a crunch of sheer agony. I swear I literally saw stars and for a moment I could do nothing but stand there, my hand going up to my jaw to massage the pain.

'You wanna fuckin go like? Got a fuckin death wish man go ed, wanna see it like, what ya got? Next wun'l tek yer ed off its shulders like!'

Understanding very little of this, I said 'You fucking arsehole! I give you a cigarette and this is how you repay me. You fucking cunt!'

'Oh wan another one like, yeah? Do you want your pizzas back?' he said raising the pizzas.

I foolishly looked down at the pizza boxes and received another blow – which I later discovered broke my jaw. It felt like I had been hit by a sledgehammer and in that moment I decided that if he hit me again he could knock me out and possibly relieve me of my pizzas *and* my wallet.

So, I went for him.

As I made a rush for him, I could see by the expression on his face that I had caught him off guard. He staggered backwards into the railings that lined the side of the road. Unfortunately he managed to get his bearings back in time to see my fist hurtling towards his face and moved his head to the side just in time. Seeing this all happen in slow motion, I took advantage of the situation and, with my free hand I took hold of his head and began to force it down towards the railings, punching his head with my other fist repeatedly as I did so. I had never had a fight before, didn't really know how to fight, but knew I had to do anything I could to beat this guy before he took me down. He had already broken my jaw and now that I had hit him he was likely to really do me over if I let him. So I kept hitting him in the head and forcing him down. I felt a sudden surge of pain and a crunch as I missed his face and my fist connected with the cold metal of the railings that lined the road, but I was now too wired and too scared to stop so I continued beating the man down until he was on the floor. He was precisely as tough as he looked and though I must have hit him about twenty times by the time he was on the floor, he still threatened to get up. So, and I feel *slightly* guilty about this, I started kicking him in the stomach and as I did so lifted my head up with the sudden realization that all of this was happening in full view of all of the cars going past on the main road. A car passed us with two children in the back seat, avidly pointing out of the window at me and shouting to their parents as I continued to kick the hoodie as if we were performing slapstick comedy. This is mainly what bought me back to my senses, and, thank god for those children, because, if they hadn't been there I don't know how long I might have continued to kick the man, such was the intensity of my fear and will to survive. Fortunately, the hoodie was still alive and even now still trying to get back to his feet. In order to ensure that he would not come after me once I turned my back I decided

I had to make this bastard really know that I had beaten him, make him fear me. So I got down on my hands and knees and, looking directly into his eyes, I hooked two fingers into his nostrils and pulled his nose back until he yelled out. Then, pointing in his face, I said in the deepest growl I could muster, 'Don't ever fuck with me again!'

All he could do was nod, and I knew I had won.

Still trembling with adrenaline, I picked up the pizzas from where they had fallen to the floor and just about managed to stand up on shaky legs.

But the ordeal wasn't over yet.

As I turned around to walk back to Terry's house I heard a loud, high pitched shriek and turned around just in time to see a young girl swinging a shopping bag through the air, which abruptly hit me in the face. In fact, it hit me just where *he* had hit me, sending fresh shockwaves through my tortured jaw.

Shaken but somehow keeping my balance, I stood in awe as the girl snatched the pizzas out of my hands - as if *I* was the one who had stolen them.

That was it, I had really had enough; battered and bruised I grabbed the girl by the arm and shoved her without thinking back into the busy road. Fortunately for her - and me - there was no traffic coming at that instant and she was able to dodge back to the pavement before getting hurt.

In the time it took this little exchange to take place, the beaten hoodie had managed to stagger to his feet and he now half stood, using the railing to balance himself.

In order to avoid turning my back on him, I said, 'Why did you do it, eh?'

He looked up at me with a pained expression. 'You shagged my girlfriend.'

Slightly surprised but wanting to maintain the position of power I had fought hard for, I looked at the now shaking girl – who I hadn't shagged - and said, 'She's a fucking trout mate, I wouldn't touch her with yours!'

'Well, my mates told me you did.' Retorted the hoodie, spitting out blood onto the pavement as he did so.

At this moment I did one of the stupid things I have ever done. I don't know if it was the massive dose of adrenaline coursing through my veins or the anger caused by the sheer assaultiveness of this pair's tag team attack but for some reason I said, 'Right, take me to your mates then. I want to talk to these fuckers!'

'Eh?' questioned the hoodie, clearly thinking that I must be a complete psycho and perhaps, that I was even more dangerous than his bruises would suggest. I hoped that this was the case, but then he said 'Ok' and began walking.

Like a fool I followed him, I had to though, if I relinquished now I might lose the upper hand and he might think I was weak. Fortunately though, my ruse paid off and he momentarily turned back towards me, looking confused before turning around again and taking a few more paces. For a moment I was concerned that I might have given him brain damage, his disorientation seemed so severe, but then he turned back towards me and did something I did not expect: he shook my hand and then went on his way.

Fortunately for me his *mates*, if they ever existed, were not waiting around the corner so I'm guessing the hoodie had counted his losses and decided that there was nowhere else he could take the situation without engaging me once again in a fight that, judging by his current state and injuries, he would probably lose.

I stood and watched him leave for a moment, the adrenaline slowly abating as a vicious pain stabbed at my jaw. Somehow I had won a fight against an adversary that was twice as big as me and probably twice as experienced in fighting.

At that moment, despite the pain, I felt as strong as a lion.

- Goodman & Goliath -

Arriving back at Terry's bedsit, I knocked on the door and was confronted with Terry's snarling face.

'Where the hell have you been, Hems?' He said, and then his face changed, and for a moment he looked a little afraid of me. I don't know what he had seen, maybe it was the blood on my fists, or maybe it was the expression of steely determination that remained on my face.

He was lost for words for a moment so I just barged past him into the hall, heading for the kitchen.

'What's happened, Hemsy?' said Terry, this made me halt for a moment, his voice and address slightly more respectful than ever before. He had called me *Hemsy* instead of, *Hems*. I hated the way he called me Hems, he said it the way a dog owner would talk to their dog when they were in a bad mood.

Reaching the kitchen, I shoved some of the post and rubbish that littered the table to the side and set down the pizzas. Then I made my way to the sink and calmly poured myself a glass of water.

'Seriously, Hemsy, what happened? Why are your hands covered in blood, what have you *done*?'

By this time, Bob had made his way into the kitchen and was now also looking at me with the same concerned expression.

'Just give me a minute guys.' I said, gargling some water and wincing as my jaw clicked loudly.

'Aooow! Mother fucker!' I said, spitting blood tinged water into the sink.

'What the hell happened to you, Hemsy?' said Bob.

'Here are your pizzas, I'll tell you while you eat.'

And so I summarised the ordeal as they ate, captivated.

'Didn't know you had it in you, Hemsy.' Said Bob, still a little shocked.

'Yeah, you're actually starting to freak me out a bit, Mark,' *Mark?* I thought - It appeared that I now ranked amongst my fellow humans. 'First you give me a sock to the old jabber box and then you go and beat up some little hoodie.'

'He was hardly little, Terry, he was bigger than you.'

He didn't like that one bit, for if I had proven that I could take down someone bigger than him then that might suggest that I could also beat him.

'Yeah, right, Hems, well you would say that wouldn't you. I bet he was just a skinny little ten year old or something.'

I just looked at him coldly.

'I don't know, Terry, I think old Hemsy is finally starting to stand up for himself. Good on you mate.'

'Thanks Bob. Only trouble is I think the bastard broke my jaw and, when I was punching him in the face I accidentally slipped and punched the railing pretty hard. Check this out.'

I raised my right fist and revealed that my rightmost small knuckle now lay about a centimetre below where it should have been.

Bob winced, 'that looks nasty man'.

'Yeah, but the thing I'm really pissed off about is the fact that I've been trying to eat this pizza for the past half hour and don't stand a chance with this jaw. It's majorly mashed.'

As if proving the point, I bit down a little and produced a loud clicking sound.

'Oooh that sounds nasty, Hems, that's gonna give you jip as you get older you know, you'll probably need to get a jaw replacement.'

For a moment I considered that and then said, 'Shut up, Terry.'

Terry grimaced and for a fleeting moment looked enraged and I could see that he contemplated giving me one of his signature prods to the ribs, but then, perhaps remembering what had happened the last time he tried that, he stormed off into the living room.

Bob watched him leave. 'Dunno what's wrong with him.'

'Probably just Pre Menstrual Terry' I said and we both laughed.

'So I take it you don't want to go out any more then Hemsy?' said Bob helping himself to my pizza now he realized that I could no longer eat it.

'Erm, actually I still want to go, just need to freshen up a bit and I'll be fine.'

'Hardcore, Hemsy,' he said, 'in fact think I might start calling you that, or no wait, Rocky!'

'Hey Terry, you coming out?' I shouted.

'No thanks, *Rocky*', said Terry clearly not happy.

'How come?' I said.

'Well someone's gotta fix these stairs for a start after you bloody hooligans have smashed the place up.'

'Unbelievable' said Bob.

'Ok mate, well we're gonna hit the town so maybe catch up with you tomorrow yeah?'

'Yeah, whatever, Hems.'

Making our way to the centre of town, I took a brief pit stop to freshen up, which meant washing the blood off my hands and face and getting changed into my new 'Spirit of Harmony' t-shirt. My jaw r*eally* ached now and part of me wished that I had just come home to bed, but a more significant part of me was feeling invigorated and more confident than I had ever felt in my life. After decking the hoodie I felt like I could do anything, which also included chatting up the cute painted toes girl. With this in mind, I took one last look in the mirror and doused myself in a knock off Calvin Kline aftershave that I had purchased from Scouser Steve.

'You look beautiful sweetheart,' said Bob.

'Thanks honey bunch.' I said.

'Let's hit the town.'

If only I had known just how hard it would hit *me.*

After stopping off at the cash point and withdrawing thirty pounds, the first port of call was the *Old Rectory*. This was one of my favourite bars as it reminded me of the set of TFI Friday, which subsequently reminded me of *Ocean Colour Scene's, Three Colours Red*. Though it was a Tuesday night there was still quite a few people on the town, though we got served pretty quickly. There was a new drink that me and Bob had acquired quite a taste for when clubbing, a vodka *Mule*: Served in a bronze bottle, it was a delicious mixture of vodka, lime and ginger and, coupled with several shots of *After Shock*, it was the perfect way to mask the pain of the possibly broken jaw and knuckle.

After downing quite a few of these concoctions we were filled with enough Dutch courage to make our way to *Larry's*.

Larry's was a dive, really. It was a meat market crammed with mostly old tarts and young horny men. The painted toes girl was neither so why she would come here I didn't know, until I got inside. It was the music. The DJ was playing an eclectic mix of *The Prodigy, Chemical Brothers*, Indy and some good dance tunes. So, after ordering another couple of mules Bob and I hit the dance floor with gusto.

Night train was playing, always a crowd pleaser, followed by *The funk soul brother.* I loved this shit.

When I noticed the painted toes girl at the other end of the dance floor I was already half cut and my world, for the second time that day, went into slow motion.

She was wearing an emerald dress, cut short to reveal shapely thighs, a tantalizing temptation of what lay above. Everything about her was sex personified, passion seeming to ooze from every pore, in perfect synchrony with my lust.

Imbued with enough Dutch courage to kill a small horse I strode over to the girl and, placing my hands on her waist I began to move my hips in time to her movements. She looked around and when she saw that it was me, she seemed to melt into me. It was a moment of heaven in a world that lately had seemed to be ruled by hell.

As *I've had the time of my life* began to play we sprang into *Dirty Dancing* mode. Sometimes it was quite useful having an older sister as you got to know all of the things that girls liked, and most of them liked the 1987 classic, *Dirty Dancing*. Fortunately for me I had watched the film enough times to have a good grasp of the moves and, it seemed, so had painted toes girl. We danced in perfect synchrony with one another and a circle began to part around us as I lifted her up and spun her through the air. She looked at me with glistening eyes and a seductive smile on her face and I seized the moment: Placing her down on the ground I cupped her face in my hands and kissed her fully, caressing her tongue in mine. She pulled back and hesitated for a moment as if considering, but then kissed back just as firmly.

Out of nowhere I felt a powerful grip take hold of my shoulder and I was pulled backwards violently. It was like being ripped from a pleasant dream. I was swung around to find my face inches away from a snarling Goodman, Flint's housemate.

'You!' he screamed.

Ah, maybe Bob had been right – Goodman was her boyfriend after all.

He pushed me back, hard, and I sprawled into some unfortunate middle aged women who appeared to be on a hen night.

'Oi, watch it love!' One of them yelled but Goodman, enraged, barged her out of the way, eager to get at me.

'Whoa there', I said, holding up my hands, 'sorry man, I had no idea.'

'Like fuck you didn't!' he said, coming towards me like a freight train. I managed to avoid his punch by dodging to the side at the last minute, which was unfortunate for Goodman as, instead of hitting me he punched the guy behind me, and that guy was *massive*. When the man turned around my first thought was that he would make a great Bond villain - he reminded me of *Jaws* - the 7ft giant with steel teeth. This guy wasn't quite that scary, but he wasn't far off.

Oblivious of the sleeping monster he had just awoken with a punch in the head, Goodman attempted to push past the man, but the goliath was having none of it. Just as Goodman was about to try and hit me again, two enormous hands picked him off the floor and threw him through the air. He landed with a yelp, connecting with a nearby table - but the giant wasn't finished yet.

'I'm not even gonna use my fists, I'm just gonna slap the shit out of you!' said the giant and he proceeded to do just that.

By this time a circle had cleared around the pair and Goodman could do nothing as the giant repeatedly slapped him in the face with enormous shovel like hands. As I watched I almost felt sorry for Goodman, who's pride was clearly taking a big dent as he was ridiculed in front of half of the town. As the bouncers finally got to the scene to cart off both men, I melted into the background but Goodman's eyes found me in the crowd as he passed. Though the bouncer was doing a good job of holding his arms behind his back, he managed to slide his hand to his neck in a neck slitting gesture clearly aimed at me.

Great. I really had to stop making enemies in this small town.

In the chaos I had completely forgotten about Bob, where was he while all this was going on? Looking around I saw him walking towards me, a deep frown on his face.

'You alright, Bo...' I began before noticing that Flint was walking behind him.

'Oooh your gonna pay for that worm boy.' Said Flint, looking at me and smiling, 'Goodman don't take kindly to people trying to dick his bird right in front of im!'

'I didn't know it was his bird!' then wondering why Bob hadn't said anything I said, 'Bob, you alright mate.'

He nodded down to his side and I followed his gaze. Flint was holding a pen knife to his kidney.

'Just making sure things was done fair boys', said Flint and he casually slipped the knife back into the inside pocket on his leather jacket.

'Looks like I should have took hold of that fucking monster instead though init.' He said, gesturing to the giant who dwarfed the bouncer.

Now that the blade had been removed from his side, Bob broke free of Flint and turned to face him, fury painted on his face, enhanced by the red disco lights.

'Tut tut' said Flint, 'I wouldn't get any ideas big man, not with the filth behind you.'

Bob looked behind him and saw that Flint was telling the truth, the police had arrived to arrest Goodman and the giant.

'Well, I'll catch up with you ladies later.' Said Flint, reaching over and playfully slapping Bobs face like a lion taunting its prey.

'You can bet on it.' Said Bob.

Flint raised his thick eyebrows and laughed humourlessly as he walked past us. When he reached the door he turned around and mimed shooting us both before laughing like this was the funniest thing in the world.

'Fucking dick!' said Bob.

'Yep. Nob.'

'I was talking about you, Hems. What the fuck were you thinking, eh?'

I was slightly stunned. 'Look I'm sorry alright, I didn't know did I?'

'I *told* you that was his fucking missus!'

'I know, I should have listened to you, but I just got overwhelmed man – she is so *fine*! Talking of which, where is she?'

'Are you fucking kidding me? Do you realize what you've just done, Hems? Goodman's just been arrested because of *you* so now he's going to spend the night in the nick with just two things on his mind. One: His missus, with your tongue down her throat and, Two: All of the ways he's going to put you in a world of pain!'

'I can handle Goodman.' I said, trying to sound tough.

'Well unfortunately it's not that simple is it, cos when you pick a fight with Goodman, you pick a fight with Flint, not to mention his fucking gangsta posse. Anyway, let's get the fuck out of here – I need a spliff!' he said, pushing me back towards the exit.

'Oh great!' he said, coming face to face with painted toes girl.

'Hey.' I said.

She looked into my face, mascara lining her cheeks and gave me an odd look before giving me a kiss. Then abruptly, she withdrew mid kiss and slapped me hard around the face.

'No!' she said, pointing a long fingernail in my face and backing away onto the dance floor. She was clearly high on something, probably ecstasy by the look of her eyes. I hadn't noticed it when were dancing because I was so carried away. I watched her dance for a moment and considered following her onto the dance floor. Then I came to my senses - Bob was right - this was insanity!

I looked to my right and Bob had left, the door still closing behind him.

I glanced back towards the girl one last time before making my way out of *Larry's* and into the night. As I left I looked at my watch and was not at all surprised to see that it was twenty two minutes past two.

I looked left and right for Bob but he had gone.

'Great!' I uttered under my breath and decided to make my way back home. I reached the seafront and a full moon seemed to beckon me to the beach, where the slow waves helped to calm my muddled mind.

I sat on cold sand and gulped in the fresh sea air. Over to my right was a small group of teenagers, probably getting drunk and partying. I tried to focus on them but couldn't – I'd had five too many mules and all I could make out were lights and shimmery figures in the distance.

'Fucking pisshead.' I said and laughed as I took out a gnarled packet of Sovereigns. As I placed one of Terry's *Death sticks* in my mouth my jaw clicked and sent fire up through my face causing me to grimace.

Jeez, what a day. What a *week*! Then I remembered I had to work tomorrow and wondered how I was going to manage with what was likely to be a massive hang over on top of a mashed jaw and a pulverised hand. I should probably get myself checked really but there was no time now. Plus I felt truly exhausted. I gazed out to sea and told myself to chill out, which wasn't hard: the moonlight danced over the sea and looked incredibly tranquil. In fact, because of the copious amounts of alcohol I had consumed I realized I was in danger of nodding off right there on the beach, which would be a bit daft considering I lived just up the road. So, I finished my cigarette and was about to get up when I saw four figures approaching from the esplanade.

Shit, it must be Goodman and Flint, I thought and chided myself for just sitting out on the beach in the open when I was clearly in some danger after the night's events.

Quickly scanning the faces in the poor light I relaxed as I realized that neither Flint nor Goodman was amongst them. Then I saw a face that I *did* know from somewhere. And then it dawned on me, far too late, that it was the hoodie I had beaten up earlier.

Roughly lifting me to my feet, the hoodie had a big smile on his face. 'Would ya look oo it is, like!' he said, putting his arm around me. For a moment I thought that maybe I had earned his respect earlier and that maybe now he wanted to be my friend. And then he got me in a headlock and punched me in the head with what felt like a brick.

'Thought you'd got away with it didn't ya ya little fuck!' he said, twisting me around and pushing me back to the floor. I didn't have time to put my hands out in front of me so my face contacted hard with the cold sand of the beach.

'Arrr' I winced, and as I raised my head, one of the hoodies friends, a tall man with long hair and a goatee, kicked me in the face. My head snapped back and my nose cracked. I felt a thick fluid running down my throat and tasted metal. I had to get out of here - I tried to get up and one of the other men kicked me in the stomach. Arching over with the pain, I curled up in a ball as the others joined in to rain blows from all sides. All I could do was hold on and try to protect my face and genitals. As if reading my mind, I felt a foot connect with my crotch and cried out with pain as my attackers laughed.

The blows seemed to go on and on.

'Alright, alright lads, think he's had enough.' Said someone, but another kick came to my head.

'Hey, hey, enough – you'll fucking kill him!'

'Yeah?'

There was a pause for a moment and then the hoodie said, 'So, you had enough then, *Spirit of Harmonee*?'

Slowly, I managed to raise my head off the ground, blood dripping onto my hands. I looked up and saw eight hazy silhouettes, though I was sure that there were only four of them.

'Fuck you!' I said and spat blood at the feet of the hoodie. I seemed to be developing something of a skill for saying and doing stupid things. Before I could look up at the hoodies face to gauge his reaction, something hit me in the face and everything went very dark.

I awoke to the smell of white musk and felt cold thighs pressing down around my chest. For a moment I thought I was having another nightmare featuring the Teresa-creature but then I felt warm kisses on my chest and mouth and knew it was painted toes girl - I really had to learn her name. I opened my eyes and looked into her face. She was still wearing the emerald dress and I could make out the shape of her breasts through the thin material.

'What's your name, love?' she said.

I tried to say my name but my mouth seemed to be filled up with something - must have just been bed mouth. I swallowed and tried again.

'Mark, what's yours?' I said.

I looked up and saw that she had been distracted by something on TV. Must have been some crime drama or something, lots of blue flashing lights and paramedics.

'Can you open your eyes for me please?' she said getting off my chest.

What? I thought and then she slapped me round the face – *hard*.

'What are you doing?' I said and she pointed in my face, before slapping me again.

'Can you hear me, come on, wake up!' she said, slapping me again.

The bed began to rise and I looked through the ceiling at the moon. Something wasn't quite right here and when

I looked down again, the bed was gone, replaced with a stretcher. I was being carried off the beach onto an ambulance.

'Can you hear me, Mark?' said a paramedic.

I nodded.

'Try and stay awake for me ok?' she said.

I nodded before once again losing consciousness.

- Purgatory -

The next couple of hours were like a series of short films recorded on an old video tape - fuzzy and incoherent snippets of scenes perforated by intermittent blackness. One minute I was gliding through space, entranced by the sparkler trails that shone through the rain swept window of an ambulance; the next, my senses were bombarded with bright lights and excruciatingly loud noise as I was wheeled through a hospital corridor on a trolley.

I shut my eyes tightly against the world, but the world was having none of it.

'Stay awake for me please', said a loud voice in my ear. 'Hello! You need to wake up now please.'

I tried to ignore the voice but it wouldn't go away. I was shaken hard by the shoulder and I opened my eyes, half expecting to see Goodman's snarling face. Instead I saw the face of a female nurse, eyes cold and uncompromising.

I squinted under the harsh intensity of the hospital lights and my head throbbed, threatening to explode.

'Can you tell me your name, please?' said the nurse.

I tried to speak and ended up coughing, blood spluttering out of my mouth and nose.

'Ark' I managed to blurt, and after the effort it took I thought I'd better take a little nap, so I closed my eyes again.

'Mark! Mark! I'm sorry but I need you to stay awake for me, please!'

The world suddenly went red as I received a hard slap to the face, igniting fresh pain in my nose and jaw.

'Aaaowww! Sheshush, what's wrong with you?' I cried.

'Can you tell me if you've taken any drugs tonight?'

Still half asleep, I couldn't bring to mind the night's events at all and just trying to remember made me feel nauseous and dizzy.

'No, don't think so.' I managed to say, before closing my eyes again.

I received another hard slap, and again, the lightning pain soared through my face. *Couldn't she see that I had already received enough blows to the face?*

'Wha, why won't you ler me sheep?' I pleaded, actually crying and then added. 'Bitch!'

'Just keep your eyes open for me please.'

I tried to keep my eyes open, but as the trolley was wheeled beneath a seemingly endless parade of burning floodlights I suddenly felt as if I were on a roller coaster and my stomach churned. I closed my eyes again to try to control the nausea and received yet another slap in the face.

Immediately, a warm torrent of fire exited my mouth in the nurse's direction. I was able to keep my eyes open long enough to see her shake the putrid liquid off her hands, the front of her scrubs soiled.

'Fucking junkies.' She said under her breath.

That'll teach you, I thought - not realizing that she had probably saved my life.

I trudged through the snow, my arms wrapped tightly against my chest as I battled the blizzard. I had no idea how long I had been travelling through this wasteland but was sure that if the onslaught didn't abate soon I may well become a frozen testament to a long forgotten race. I was worried about my legs more than anything – *why were they so cold?* Looking down I discovered the answer – I didn't appear to be wearing any trousers, or for that matter, any underwear! *How could that be? Why was I walking through the snow half naked and why did the back of my hand hurt so much?*

I held out my hand to investigate and felt something hard and alien embedded in my flesh. *What the hell?*

I opened my eyes and the blizzard disappeared, fractionally. I found myself in a strange white room where the sound of the blizzard seemingly continued but the snow had stopped. Still holding the back of my hand, I discovered a plastic catheter plug and things slowly started coming back to me.

I was in the hospital, that much was clear, but looking around I also discovered the source of the blizzard and the reason for the cold: a large window was standing wide open with a gust of cold air howling and whistling its way to the bed where I lay half naked in a paper night gown.

My body shivered and I tried to get some warmth from the flimsy blanket. Surveying the room some more I noticed a large clock on the far wall and saw that it was five thirty seven in the morning.

My immediate thought was to return to sleep, but I was still only vaguely aware of how I had gotten here and knew that if I wanted to go back to sleep I would first have to leave behind the relative sanctity of the blanket and go and close the window. Judging by the time I guessed that some overzealous nurse had opened the window at five thirty as an attempt to possibly invigorate (or kill) the half naked residents. What sort of person would do that? Then I had a flashback to the happy slapper nurse who I had involuntarily vomited over. Maybe this was her way of getting back at me.

Opening my eyes again I summoned all of my will to make a move to the window and began to raise my head off the pillow.

That was when the first real pain hit me. It was like waking up from the worst hangover of your life – every tiny movement like a lead weight crushing my skull. After my initial attempt I lay back down again and just held my head for a long time. Then after a while the pain started to dissipate somewhat and I became aware of the pain in my nose and jaw instead.

'Jesus.' I whispered. *What the hell happened to me?* I thought back and remembered the nightclub, the girl, Goodman! Did I get into a fight with Goodman? Then I remembered Flint holding a knife to Bob's kidney. Jesus if they did this to me what had they done to Bob? Then I remembered the giant and the police carting Goodman off, the throat slitting gesture as he left. Did he get out and do me over? Unlikely. But how did I end up in this state. *Think!* I thought. I was able to rekindle fragments of memory, and then I recalled quite clearly sitting on the beach and smoking a Sovereign. But nothing else.

As I lay there I realized that I really needed to take a leak and decided that despite the pain, I was going to have to brave a trip to the toilet.

Before I could move, an Indian man in a white coat appeared next to my bed, who I presumed must be a doctor.

'Mr Hems?' he said.

'Yes?' I croaked.

'Good morning – I'm Doctor Riaz. It's good to see you awake. We were a little concerned about you there for a while but we were able to bring you out of intensive care last night.'

'Intensive care?' I said.

'Yes,' he said walking around the bed and withdrawing a small pen-light, 'you were bought in here in the early hours of Wednesday morning and you may be surprised to discover that it is now *Thursday* morning.

'Whoa, sorry that was a bit lazy'. I said and winced at the pain in my jaw.

He laughed at that and said, 'No, no – you needed the rest, you have sustained quite some injuries, mostly minor, but we'll go through that in a moment. First, let's take a look at you. Now I'm just going to shine a light into your eyes – if you could just look at me please'.

I fought the pain and focussed on his large brown eyes and thick eyebrows as he shone the light in my eyes.

'Ok, that's good.' He said, putting cold fingers on my neck glands.

'Do you have any loss of vision, headaches, anything like that?'

'I've got a pretty bad headache but my eyes seem to be ok.' I said closing and opening my eyes and testing their focussing capabilities.

'Well, that's to be expected', he said, 'now I'd like you to look at my pen and just follow it with your eyes, please.'

He slowly moved the pen from left to right and then back again, then he moved it up and down and my eyes followed.

'Ok, that's good.' He said. He walked over to the foot of the bed and picked up a chart that was clipped there, studying it, he said: 'Do you have any allergies that you are aware of?'

'No.'

He wrote some notes on the clipboard.

'Ok, I'm going to prescribe you with some painkillers that the nurse will bring for you three times a day.' He continued to write on the form and then looked back up at me and asked: 'how are your nose and jaw feeling?'

'Not great, my nose is really painful and it hurts to talk.'

He inspected my face and said: 'Well, the good news is, Mr Hems, you are alive and relatively healthy. The bad news is you have sustained a number of relatively minor injuries. Your nose is broken, you have a fractured mandible - that's the lower jaw bone, and the base knuckle of your little finger is broken. You also have some minor cuts and bruises, but besides that you have been really quite lucky.

Lucky? I thought, this guy had a strange sense of fortune.

'Ok, I will leave you in the capable hands of the nurses, but we would like to keep you under observation for a few days until you get your strength back, ok?'

'Ok' I said, feeling suddenly very tired. As the doctor walked off my head hit the pillow and I fell almost immediately back to sleep.

Waking again a few hours later I realized that I was now quite desperate to go to the toilet, so I slowly brought my legs around the side of the bed and held my head against the shockwave of pain. I sat there for a moment with my hands on my face and felt a little naked - I *was* a little naked, sitting there in nothing but the paper slip. This and the urge to pee brought me to action.

Lowering myself off the bed, my feet touched freezing cold linoleum but I couldn't stand up yet – my head was still swimming a little with the pain. *Right!* I thought. *Can't sit here all day. I've got to get out of this nightmare*. I snapped my eyes open and stood up straight, holding the bed for a moment for support, slightly disgusted at the plastic sheet on the bed.

Surveying the room again I saw that my bed was one of eight; most of the others had curtains drawn around them but the one next to mine was occupied by a man who appeared to be in his fifties and snoring. As I passed I jumped to the side a little as he suddenly coughed loudly before resuming his snoring rhythm. Ahead of me I could see a large white desk with a nurse with grey hair sitting at it. She was writing notes with a red pen. As I approached she looked up at me, her face cold and as grey as her hair. I realized that I must have looked quite pitiful standing there shivering, hugging my shoulders to stay warm.

'Can you tell me the way to the toilet please?' I croaked, my voice barely audible.

She pointed behind me and to the right and I nodded as if to say thank you before hobbling off in that direction. The gent's toilet had a wide white door with a long metal handle that I guessed was meant to be opened with your arms, to prevent sick people leaving germs everywhere. I made my way inside and locked the door behind me. I immediately began to untie the string that held the paper gown together and as I did so noticed a series of black bruises lining my legs and ribs. But there was no time to inspect those now – my bladder felt set to burst so I immediately unleashed a torrent of hot urine into the toilet and winced as I felt a slight burning sensation. I vaguely remembered being kicked in the privates and hoped I hadn't sustained any real damage to *that* part of my anatomy. Concerned but relieved, I refastened the night gown and turned around to wash my hands. Then I almost jumped back in horror at the sight that greeted me in the mirror. I would have been perfect for a role in one of George A. Romero's zombie flicks; blood lay encrusted around my mouth and nose and my eyes peered back at me through dark pits.

Despite my horrendous appearance though, I felt somehow strong; a steely determination building up inside me, urging me to pick myself up and get myself back together.

Using my wrist to turn on the faucet (the faucet had a long handle like the door) I began dabbing water at my wounds, carefully washing away the encrusted blood. It was slow and painful work but when I was done I looked a little better – still a train wreck but at least a live one!

Beginning to feel a little weak I made my way back the way I had come. On passing the large white desk, the nurse handed me a small piece of paper and a red clip board.

'While you're up, if you could just fill out what meals you would like, please. Just tick the boxes to choose what you want.'

'Thanks' I whispered, taking the form and hobbling back to my bed. I placed the form on the bed and shivered again as a gust of wind hit me from the open window. *This is ridiculous*, I thought. I looked back at the desk and saw that the nurse had disappeared so I walked over to the window and attempted to close it. It was a big old sash window and it was heavy. I had to really tug at it to bring it down and as I did so I felt the energy drain from my body. As I looked out of the window to the garden below I felt suddenly quite dizzy and had to stand there for a moment with my head against the cold glass before trying again. This time the window came down and I made my way back to the bed to try and warm myself up under the inadequate covers.

I noticed a plastic bag by the side of my bed and could see the chequered pattern of my shirt through the Tesco logo. It appeared to be covered in blood, and that, and the lack of food, made me quite queasy and I felt weak again. Hoisting myself atop the high bed, I clambered under the blanket and hugged it tightly to myself.

When I was about nine years old I used to think I saw my dead Grandad sitting at the bottom of my bed wearing a chequered suit. Though I wanted him to be, I never believed he was actually there – I'm pretty sure that I had made him up as a means of trying to find proof for something more to life than the ordinary. Even at nine years old. So when I opened my eyes to see an old man in a suit sitting at the end of my bed, my first thought was that maybe I was actually seeing a real ghost this time.

But then my eyes adjusted to the harsh white light in the hospital room and I saw that it was actually a man in a police uniform.

'Good morning, Mr...Hems?'

'Yes, good morning.' I said, my jaw cracking and making me wince.

'Ah, had to check', he said, bringing a small notebook out of his pocket and writing a quick note. 'My, you have been in the wars haven't you.' He said looking at my injuries.

'I've had better days.' I said.

'How rude of me, sorry, I'm sergeant Brown of Weymouth and Portland Police.'

'Hello.' I said.

He smiled at me in a gentle sort of way and then said: 'Mr Hems I'm here today to take a statement and some photos of your injuries. Do you feel up to that?'

I nodded, swallowing and feeling pain in my jaw and nose.

'I don't know how much help I'll be though to be honest – I can't remember very much.'

He looked at me carefully, perhaps trying to ascertain whether I was telling the truth.

'Well let's just start at the beginning shall we. What can you remember about last night?'

I thought back carefully to the events of the previous day. Start at the beginning? Well I couldn't tell him about the situation with Terry as that resulted in a broken window, and I didn't want to tell him about beating up the hoodie, although it was possible that the hoodie might have been responsible I suppose.

'All I remember,' I said, 'was going to *Larry's* with my mate, Bob...'

'Bob? Could I have this gentleman's surname please in case I need to take a statement?'

Damn, I thought, Bob wouldn't be very happy about that, not when he was usually in possession of at least an eighth of weed.

'Bainbury.' I said, 'but I'm pretty sure he wasn't there when this happened.' I pointed at my face.

'Ah, so you do remember something?'

'Well, I remember being at *Larry's* with Bob, having a few to drink, probably a few too many to be honest and then...'

I thought about the painted toes girl and the wonderful kiss we had followed by Goodman being thrown across the room by the giant. Then I thought about Flint again. Could he have had something to do with my present condition? I certainly wouldn't put it past him, he was an evil sonofabitch. But that didn't feel quite right.

'Mr Hems?' said the policeman.

'Oh, sorry, I was just trying to remember. I left *Larry's* at about...' I had a sudden vision of looking at my watch on the beach, a sovereign in my hand. The time of course was 2:22. '...about 2:20.'

'Ok, what happened next?'

I remembered looking at the moon, how tranquil it looked sitting over the black sea. Then I remembered seeing a small party of people over to my right, but they were all fuzzy in my memory.

'I remember there was a small party on the beach over to my right, probably five or six people, but I don't think they had anything to do with this.'

'Why do you say that? Do you remember who did this to you, Mr Hems?'

I thought hard. Flashes of memory came back to me. The faceless silhouettes of four men taunted me as I lay on the floor! One had long hair, but that's all I remembered.

'I remember there were four men.' I said, 'Four men did this to me on the beach...'

The policeman wrote down the words *4 assailants* in his notebook.

'Did you know any of these men, Mr Hems?'

I looked back into my memory trying to focus on the details of the men's faces, but the harder I tried the more obscured their details became.

'I don't think so.' I said, 'is it possible that they didn't know me and just saw me as an easy target – maybe they mugged me – I just realized that I don't think I have my wallet!'

'Actually, Mr Hems, your wallet was recovered from your jeans, that's how we knew your name – your bank card is still in your wallet, so I doubt theft was the motive.'

'Ah. Bang goes that theory then.' I said, genuinely perplexed.

'Do you have any enemies, Mr Hems?'

'No. I don't think so. I mean, I generally just get on with people, you know?'

'Ok, did you do anything at the nightclub that could have provided someone with a motive to follow you to the beach?'

I thought back to Goodman and Flint again. There was no way I was going to mention Flint to the police, I was already in enough trouble with his posse and that would be basically signing my own death warrant.

'What's quite interesting, Mr Hems, and this is probably pure coincidence, is that the Police were called out to *Larry's* last night to investigate a ruckus between two gentlemen, a...' he rifled a few pages back in his notebook, 'Mr John Goodman and a Mr Edward Lock. Are you familiar with either of these men?'

'...No, I'm afraid not.' I said, shaking my head.

The police man looked at me carefully and I began to feel uncomfortable under his scrutiny. He looked like he had been in the business a long time, probably knew I was lying.

'Well.' He said suddenly, flipping his notebook closed, 'Let's take some photos shall we. Not the most glamorous you will have looked I'm afraid, but necessary all the same.' He smiled, 'Are you ok to carry on?'

'Yes.' I nodded.

The truth was I was actually exhausted by the conversation. I realized that I had fallen to sleep earlier without filling out my form for breakfast so maybe the nurses had presumed I didn't want anything.

The policeman ducked below the bed and arose with an old fashioned box camera that looked like it was made of wood. It even had a separate flash bulb!

'Wow, nice camera.' I said, not actually meaning to sound sarcastic.

'Yeah,' he smiled, 'it's a bit of a relic now but when we first got this beauty, she was state of the art!'

'This is still the year two thousand, right? I didn't go back in time to the thirties or anything did I?'

'No no,' he said laughing, 'it's still the year two thousand, I'm afraid, although in some ways I wish we *were* back in the thirties – there was a lot less crime back then, I can tell you! But then, I guess I wouldn't have as much to keep me busy.'

He adjusted a plate on the back of the camera and then appeared to be ready.

'Ok, if you could just turn to the left for me please.'

'Ok' I said. As I turned my head away I noticed that he averted his eyes from the flash. It was bright!

'Ok, now if you could look forward but try not to look at the bulb ok – look at my face.'

'Ok,' I said, looking at the policeman's face. He could have actually been my grandad, and then some probably, he must have been getting on. I hoped that I was still as active at his age.

The camera flashed brightly again and left a bit of an afterimage in the periphery of my vision. It felt like there was an image in the corner of my eye that I couldn't quite make out.

'Ok, one more. If you could just turn your face to the left, please.'

I turned my face to the left and there was one more bright flash.

'Ok, that should do it.' He said, kneeling down to pack away his camera in a brown leather box.

'If anything comes back to you, please do let us know, wont you?' He said. Then, when he had finished packing away the camera he got to his feet and handed me a piece of paper with his name and a telephone number on it.

'Unfortunately we don't get given nice printed cards so this will have to do. If you think of anything, anything at all, give that number a call and ask for Sergeant Brown, ok?'

'Will do. Thanks.' I said.

'Ok. Thanks for your time, Mr Hems. Now you try to stay out of trouble won't you and don't worry, I'm sure that your face will heal and you'll be chasing all the ladies again in no time.' He said, giving me a wink before turning around and heading off towards the exit.

Yep, chasing all the ladies. I thought. I wonder if that's what had gotten me into this mess? In some ways I wished that were true because if this was somehow Goodman's doing, perhaps through Flint, then maybe Goodman would be satisfied that I had learnt my lesson.

I tried to conjure up the faces of my attackers again and simply couldn't do it. I vaguely remembered saying *Fuck you!* And trying to spit blood in their faces, but the rest was a blur.

After the policeman had left it suddenly occurred to me that I was supposed to be at work two days ago and nobody knew where I was. Padding over to the large white desk I asked the nurse if there was a phone that I could use.

'Well, I *could* tell you where the phone is, but only if you fill in your meal form first, please.' She handed over another red clipboard with a form on it. There were three options and I chose the chicken nuggets and mash, which actually sounded amazing right now.

'What time's lunch?' I said, ticking the box labelled "Option B".

'12.30 and the phone's over there,' she said, pointing down a glaring hallway.

'Thanks', I said, handing the form back to her.

I padded down the hall and confronted the phone. Hopefully I could still remember the Crows nest's number. Yep, no worries there, it was 784520. It would take a lot to dislodge that number – I had to say it virtually every day when leaving an order on the answer phone for the delivery firms.

I typed it into the phone and after a brief pause, the Duchess picked up.

'Hello, Mrs Warner .' I said.

'Mark! Where the hell have you been? You were supposed to be in yesterday and today, Gavin's had to cope on his own and, Mr Warner isn't happy, I can tell you!'

'I...' I tried to say.

'No excuses, Mark. You'll be lucky if you still have a job when you come back, now get yourself into work now, please.'

'I'm afraid I won't be able to do that, Mrs Warner .'

'What do you mean, where are you?'

'I'm in hospital. I got...mugged on the beach, got beaten up pretty bad. I lost a lot of blood so they put me in intensive care for the night. I only recovered consciousness this morning.'

There was a pause. 'Oh, well, ok. Oh dear that sounds awful - I'm sorry to hear that, Mark. Ok, you just concentrate on getting better then wont you and we'll see you when you've recovered, ok.'

'Ok, bye.'

'Bye, Mark.'

Well, that was a turn up. She actually sounded *compassionate* for a minute there! I put the phone down to sever the connection and then decided to give Bob a call.

He answered after a couple of rings. 'He...<cough> hello?' he'd probably just taken a toke on his bong.

'Hey mate.'

'Hemsy!' Where have you been? Haven't seen you since Tuesday night – thought something might have happened to you.'

'Yeah, well, something *did* happen to me.' I said.

'What do you mean? What's up?'

'Well after you left *Larry's* I went to follow you...'

'Shit, really? I thought you were just gonna hook up with that bird.'

'No, wish I had now. No, I left the club and I think I went straight to the beach for some reason.'

'Why?'

'Dunno, I can't actually remember a lot, I suppose I've got a bit of memory loss.'

'What the hell happened, Hemsy, are you ok?'

'Well, I've got a broken nose, two black eyes, cut lip, broken jaw, fucked fist and I'm walking with a bit of a limp, but apart from that I'm fine.'

'Holy shit – Hems. Fuck I'm sorry man, I shouldn't have left you. Was it Goodman, Flint?'

'I actually don't know. All I remember is that there were four men.'

'Fuck. Alright, where are you? I'll come over.'

'I'm at Weymouth hospital.'

'Ok mate, I'll be there in about half an hour.'

'Nice one mate. Oh, can you do me a favour and bring me some clothes from my place on the way please?'

'Sure. Oh, how do I get in though?'

'You can use the credit card trick, remember?'

'Oh yeah, ok. Alright, Hemsy, I'll see you soon. I'll drop by and pick up Terry on the way – think he was looking for you to go robbing with yesterday.'

'Well at least I avoided that! Ok mate, I'll see you soon.'

'Bye.' He hung up.

I decided that I desperately needed a cigarette but thought that it was unlikely that the hospital would sell them. Kind of counterproductive. Then I remembered the bag with my clothes in it. It was possible that a cigarette or two might have survived my beating. Maybe.

I padded back to my bed and picked up the plastic Tesco's bag from the floor. Opening it up I found that it was a good call to ask Bob to pick me up some clothes, I doubted I'd be able to wear these again! The jeans were covered in blood and vomit, as was my checked shirt, which was a shame – that was one of my favourites! Remarkably though, my new T shirt, the one with *Spirit of Harmony* printed on it, looked ok - only a couple of spots of blood stained it, which might wash out if I was lucky.

Tugging it out of the bag, I decided to put it on – it might help prevent me getting frostbite if the nurses kept insisting on keeping that big window open!

Next I went through the jeans pockets. In one I found my lighter and in the other I found a very battered packet of Sovereign's. Opening the packet, to my relief I saw that at least four of the cigarettes were smoke-able, possibly five, if I held that one together as I smoked.

I pushed myself off the bed again and made my way over the cold floor. For the first time in my life I wished that I had a pair of slippers. Approaching the grey nurse I asked her if there was a place I could smoke.

'Well we don't really condone that, but if you *must* you can smoke out of the window in the television room, up those stairs, first on the left.' She said pointing to a stair well down the hall.

‘Don’t forget,’ she said, ‘lunch will be served at 12.30.’

‘Ok, thanks’ I said. My voice still hushed to avoid disturbing some of the sleeping patients.

I made my way up the stairs and found the television room where the nurse said it would be. I opened a large fire door and walked into a room that I was happy to see was equipped with a thick green carpet. As I walked in I noticed a middle aged woman at the window smoking and felt a little embarrassed at my state of undress.

‘Hi there.’ I said.

She nodded and said: ‘Crikey you’ve been in the wars haven’t you!’

It was funny how everybody seemed to say that, like we were all predisposed with a script of key phrases that matched certain situations.

‘What happened to you?’ she said.

‘I er, got mugged on the beach.’ I said.

`Oooh, well at least they didn’t take your ciggies, eh?’ she said, looking at my battered pack of Sovereigns.

‘Yeah, hah, that’s true. It’s the first thing you tend to want when you’ve had the crap beaten out of you too! Feels a bit weird smoking in a hospital though.’

‘Yeah, the nurses don’t like it very much.’ She said taking a deep drag and blowing it out of the window.

I approached the window and lit one of my battered Sovereign’s, glancing out into the white day as I did so. We were on the third floor here and there was a sobering drop to the garden below, but above that was the roof of the ward I was in – a slate flat grey roof that had been tarmacked.

The roof was a giant ashtray. I mean, literally – there were hundreds if not *thousands* of cigarette butts littered all over it. This was quite ironic considering how many people were dying within the hospital walls of various cancers, and it made me feel quite guilty.

‘It’s quite a shocking sight isn’t it?’ said the woman.

‘Yeah. You’d think someone would get out there and clean them off.’

‘Maybe they don’t want to. Maybe they want to make smokers like you and I feel disgusted at ourselves.’

‘Huh – maybe your right. It’s certainly working.’ I said looking down at my cigarette. Having said this I put it in my mouth and lit it.

‘Not working *that* well then!’ she said laughing.

I laughed, ‘Well I really need this right now. Besides I’m just going to make sure I quit before I’m thirty. When you get to thirty all of your cells begin to lose their ability to regenerate, but as long as I quit a bit before thirty, then my body should repair the damage.’

‘Is that so? Well I guess I’m screwed then.’

‘Oh, sorry - I didn’t mean...’ I said, feeling embarrassed.

‘Don’t worry I’m just messing with you.’ She said, finishing her cigarette and flicking it out of the window to bounce amongst the myriad butts on the roof, like a drop in an ashy ocean.

‘See you later.’ She said, making her way towards the door.

‘Bye.’ I said, still feeling a bit awkward about my remarks. What if she were a cancer patient or something? *God, what an idiot.*

I looked out of the window and without thinking touched my nose against the glass and flinched back as fresh pain shot up my skull.

I wondered why nobody had reset my nose or cleaned my face. I guessed it must have been because I threw up over that nurse, and they seemed to think I was a junky. I would just have to deal with a bent nose from now on unless I got it fixed at some point in the future. Certainly not now – I didn't think my body could take any more pain.

Finishing my cigarette I looked at the clock and saw that it was 12.35. Damn I'd better get down for lunch or suffer the wrath of the grey nurse. So, like thousands of smokers that had gone before me, I flicked my cigarette into the butt graveyard and made my way back downstairs.

It's funny, people usually complain about hospital food, but to me the chicken nuggets, mash and peas I ate on that day was the most delicious thing I had ever tasted. Even if the pleasure was diluted some by the pain of chewing with my battered jaw. I guess it was because I was so hungry, my body craving fuel badly after not eating for what must have been a couple of days. In fact, I couldn't remember the last time I had eaten. After I finished I felt remarkably refreshed – obviously I was in a lot of pain, but now at least I felt semi human, with a warmth inside me.

Bob and Terry arrived around 1 and I saw Bob asking the grey nurse where I was. This was strange as both of them looked directly at me as they scanned the room. Eventually, the nurse pointed at me and I gave a little wave.

With eyes wide my friends approached me, mouths slightly gaping.

'Jesus Hems. What the fuck *happened* to you!'

'Dunno mate – got sort of mugged on the beach but can't really remember it.'

'Shit.', said Bob, 'I had no idea it was this bad Hemsy . God I shouldn't have left you.'

'Don't be daft man. It's not your fault. God knows what I was thinking sitting on the beach at 2 in the morning!'

'So you don't remember who did this to you then, Hems? Cos we need to pay these bastards a visit!' said Terry. His face enraged.

I thought back hard again.

'No. Hopefully it will come back at some point.'

'Well what *do* you remember?'

I told them pretty much what I had told the policeman that morning – about leaving the club, sitting on the beach smoking a Sovereign and then the four shadowy figures.

As I told them what I remembered, Bob sat on the end of the bed and Terry pulled up a cheap plastic chair.

'I bet it was Flint you know, that bloke's a psycho.'

'Yeah, he pulled a knife on Bob you know.' Said Terry.

'Yeah I know – I was there.' Looking at Bob, I said, 'Do you reckon Goodman got put in the nick that night?'

'Dunno mate, spose it's possible they might have just questioned him and let him go. Dunno though, he was going pretty mental. Usually they lock people up for the night when they're in that state.'

'True.' I said.

'Hey what about that bloke you beat up who tried to steal your pizzas?' said Terry, 'maybe it was him.'

'Yeah, could have been – I just don't know.' I said, plumping the pillow up behind me to make myself more comfortable.

Bob looked thoughtful and then seemed to remember something.

'Oh, here's your stuff by the way, Mark.' He said, passing over a plastic bag full of clothes.

'Went through your drawers and got you a few pairs of socks and pants. I didn't know what trousers and that you wanted so I just picked up your combats and a couple of t-shirts. Oh, I put your toothbrush in there as well.'

'Oh nice one buddy – you're a star.' I said having a quick look through the bag, 'it'll be nice to put some trousers on – feel nek-ed in this paper nightie!'

Looking to my right I saw that Terry had retrieved a bottle of white lightning from his bag and was swigging it down.

'What the fuck are you doing, Terry? This is a fucking hospital man – put it away!' Said Bob in a raised whisper.

Terry looked around the room and gesticulated at the other patients.

'None of these poor bastards are gonna mind, init. Probably could do with some themselves.'

'Just put it away before the nurse sees.'

Terry looked around at the grey nurse. She had her head down, oblivious. He took another long swig and then replaced the cap and burped. The nurse looked up at that and Terry quickly returned the bottle to his bag.

'Wrongun' said Bob, shaking his head.

I laughed and it hurt so I stopped abruptly and held my jaw.

'Fuck man, when we find the gibronis who did this, Mark!'

Terry nodded his head vigorously and then did a throat slitting gesture, which I *definitely* could have done without.

- Spirit of Harmony -

After Bob and Terry left I felt quite drained again so it wasn't hard to sleep. Then I was rudely awakened by the nurse (they had a tendency of doing this) who handed me two tablets and a small beaker of water.

'Take these please.' She said.

Taking the tablets I winced again as my jaw creaked. I drank all of the water down, not realizing how thirsty I had been.

'Thanks.' I said and glanced at the clock.

It was 2.22 in the afternoon.

'No!' I said out loud.

The nurse paused at the side of the bed, a perplexed expression on her face.

'Oh, sorry, erm just realized I missed my favourite TV show' I said.

Apathetic, the nurse walked over to the next patient to continue her rounds.

My attention returned to the clock. *What was it with those numbers?* This was getting way beyond weird now.

How many times had I seen 222 recently? Five, six times a day maybe? Surely that sort of frequency was considerably beyond the limits of coincidence?

As I pondered this, I propped myself up on my pillow and as I did so looked down at the symbols on my t-shirt – the Yin Yang symbol, the Cross and the six pointed star or star of David. *Why had I bought this again?* I wondered, then as I studied the Yin Yang symbol, something occurred to me. It was made up of two opposing forces – black and white - one within the other. I looked at the next symbol and it was made up of two opposing lines - horizontal and vertical. Then I looked at the third symbol. It was a star of David. Ah, I guess it would have been too much of a coincidence. But as I studied the symbol I realized that it was made up of two opposing triangles, one pointed up and one pointed down.

I felt slightly stunned, the slow realization of the possible connection between the numbers and symbols having the feeling of an epiphany as a shiver rose up my spine and my scalp tingled.

I decided I wanted to have a cigarette and think about this some more so I leaned over to pick up my Sovereigns and brought my legs out from beneath the blanket. It was still quite cold, so I decided to put on my combat trousers. As I started to pull them on I realized that there was a weight in one of the pockets. *The Tarot cards!* They might actually help me to figure out the connection between the numbers and the symbols, if indeed there was one. I buttoned up my combats and pulled out the tarot box containing the deck together with the handy tarot guide before making my way up to the TV room.

There was nobody up there this time, which was good as I didn't want to look like a weirdo with my Tarot deck. Dropping the Tarot on to one of the cheap plastic chairs I went to the window and lit up.

Could it be that this was all part of one big sign of some sort? I mean, I knew it was clutching at straws but hadn't the t-shirt felt destined for me from the beginning? The moment I first saw it I felt that it was special in some way - maybe this was why. Maybe it was like the Tarot? I once read that the Tarot was based on *synchronicity* – the Jungian notion that there may be a governing dynamic that underlies the whole of human experience, that *supersedes* the physical laws of cause and effect. A system expressed by the conscious mind's ability to see between the lines and make connections from meaningful coincidences. Certainly the sheer frequency of seeing this particular sequence of numbers – 222, was well beyond normal coincidence. Or was it? Maybe I was just going mad. Perhaps, in my desire to find meaning in the Universe I was fabricating it. Then I remembered the mini advert. The numbers shining thirty feet high from the cinema screen.

No way! There was something going on here – these things were *not* figments of my imagination; they had happened, they were real, and if they were coincidences, then who's to say that they weren't meaningful ones. I thought back over everything I had witnessed recently; the gypsy and the coins, the clocks, the shop signs, the mini advert, and possibly the t-shirt. Taking one last drag on my cigarette, I flicked it out onto the ashtray of a roof, and blew out smoke in a long grey plume.

Synchronicity. I thought and picked up the tarot deck. As the tarot was all about synchronicity, maybe it could provide me with some answers. Opening the box, I pulled out the deck and reverentially laid it to one side. Then I pulled out the book and started rifling through it. The first thing that caught my attention was a section on The Qabalah and Tarot symbolism. There was a picture of the 'Tree of Life' and a description that read:

Everything is connected. There are 22 letters in the Hebrew alphabet, 22 Tarot cards in the major arcana and 22 paths in the Tree of Life.

More 2's! I thought, but maybe that was taking it too far.

I turned the page and got a prickly feeling at the nape of my neck as I saw four triangles with lines intersecting them at various points. Beneath each one was the name of one of the elements: Earth, Air, Fire and Water.

The passage beneath read:

The ability to read and make sense of the Tarot is underpinned by a solid grounding in the esoteric symbols reflected time and again in the various systems of the Occult. One of the most important symbols is the Triangle. The Triangle was used to represent one of the four elements of the ancient world: Earth, Air, Water and Fire. It was believed that everything in the Universe was made up of these four elements with a fifth element emerging when all four elements work together in harmony to create a kind of alchemy. The fifth element is known as the quintessence, an element that appears to transcend the physical Universe and may be synonymous with the soul.

Below this there was a depiction of the four triangles interlocked, which to my awe created a six pointed star, a star of David. I looked down at my t-shirt, *Spirit of Harmony,* and saw the star reflected there. Another co-incidence.

Turning the page, there was a set of astrological symbols that I was relatively familiar with. All fairly common Occult stuff. I turned the next page however and saw a picture of a Yin Yang symbol and a description:

The T'ai Chi Tu or Yin Yang is a product of Taoist philosophy. It represents duality, with the opposing black and white forces contained within a circle (a symbol of unity) yet also embodied within one another. The perfect marriage and harmony of opposites. Some scholars have gone on to suggest that the Yin Yang is also symbolic of the balance between heaven and hell, where man's experience on earth (or hell) is represented by the white within the black. Subsequently, on passing over to the next world (heaven) the soul's experience of the world is represented as the black circle within the white.

I was in awe. Whether the events that had led me to reading this were extraordinary or simply ordinary, it didn't matter, I felt like I was discovering fundamental truths about the Universe. Excited I read on, hoping to find the third image on my t-shirt - a picture of a cross. But I couldn't find one. Instead there was just a small section on symbols derived from the Enochian system, which seemed to be quite similar to the elemental triangles I had seen earlier, albeit in a slightly different form. Following this, the book started to go into the meanings associated with the cards of the Tarot. I began to page through them and first of all came to *The Fool* and once again marvelled at the marked resemblance to Terry. Then I turned the page and saw *The magician*.

Making ideas into reality. I thought.

This was the card that supposedly represented my present in the brief Tarot reading I had at Bob's house.

I was about to turn the page but then I noticed the two Yin Yang symbols, one next to each of the magicians hands.

A snake like shiver slithered up my back.

Everything's connected, I thought, *My wishes, the 2's, the symbols*. But what did it mean? I read the description of the card:

The magician stands between the pillars of light and darkness, night and day, between the Qabalistic paths of severity (Geburah) and mercy (Chesed), squarely positioned on the middle, or Christ, path. The halo behind the magician's head echoes this holy position and the balance between heaven and earth inherent in man is reflected in the Yin Yang symbols presented next to the hands of the Magus. Logos (The Word) is also presented on the card, cementing the Magician as the second member of the Christian Trinity: The Son.

I wondered if the other symbols would have similar meanings so I scanned through the pages searching for a star, Yin Yang symbol or cross.

I stopped at the *Strength* card, partly because this had been the card that represented the past in my tarot reading and partly because of the dream where I turned into a lion, which in turn reflected one of my wishes.

Two rays of light were cast inwards from the corners of the card to intersect at the centre, creating an inverted triangle. This sat on top of another triangle containing a circle and a woman at prayer. It was almost like a magic eye picture - you didn't see it right away but when you studied it for a while, a star of David was clearly revealed.

For a few moments I remained transfixed, beads of sweat dripping down the side of my face. Feeling like I was pushing against a momentous weight, I read the description that appeared beneath the image:

The Strength card presents a flame haired woman, indicative of a lioness, summoning the creative forces that emanate from the spirit. She sits at the centre of a six pointed star where the four elements intersect to create the quintessence of the soul. As with card 1, The

> *Magician, the Strength card can be linked to the Christian Trinity as it represents the third member, the Holy Ghost.*

I need a cigarette, I thought and went back over to the window. The air felt heavy around me and I suddenly felt that there was hidden meaning in every atom of every thing. I was afraid to look out of the window in case I saw a dove or a shooting star or maybe three giant two's in the sky! Fortunately there was nothing but the garden a couple of floors below and that same misty whiteness that had seemed to cling to the world for the last few days. I remembered the gypsy woman walking into that mist and disappearing from my view, taking with her all of her mysteries.

Until now, perhaps.

I looked at the cigarette and put it back into the pack. I was too eager to find out more. Walking back over to the chair, I picked up the Tarot book and moved on past the *Strength* card. I had already found the Yin Yang symbol and the star but if I also discovered the cross, then maybe this would be the final piece of the jigsaw puzzle.

Something nagged at the back of my mind and I was sure I had seen a cross in the Tarot before, but where? As I searched each Tarot card, I couldn't find one. There were lots of astrological symbols but so far no crosses, which seemed quite unusual given what a common symbol it was.

As I approached the end of the book, my excitement began to diminish and I felt sure that I would not find the final symbol. After all this was reality - the likelihood of all of these elements coming together like some cosmic codex was highly improbable. It was with this thought that I reached the final page.

There was no cross.

Feeling deflated, I checked that there were no further pages before turning back to the final page.

This page was all about the final Tarot card in the major arcana, No. 21, *The Universe*. Because it was such an abstract card I had forgotten that it had also come up in my Tarot reading, as the future. The card depicted four interlocking qabalistic trees – each representing a different dimension of the Universe. I was quite familiar with the Qabalah so I was used to seeing it as a single tree, but when you put it together like this....

It became a cross!

My heart leapt, my mind buzzed and the fine hairs at the back of my neck prickled. *How had I not seen this immediately?* Perhaps it was because I was so familiar with the finer detail of the tree of life – the individual elements (or sephiroth) that composed it that I had literally failed to see the bigger picture.

Now it was clear as day.

I felt very cold now and my breathing was a little erratic. I wanted to go downstairs and put another t-shirt on but I felt that I was on the verge of an earth shattering discovery and I was rooted to the spot. I *had* to read on. Underneath the image was written:

The Universe, Great One of the night of Time, is represented as a tree of life for each of the four worlds, Assiah, Briah, Atziluth and Yetzirah all interconnected via a central sephiroth, Kether, from which all life in the Universe emanates. This card indicates the omnipresent, omniscient and eternal nature of existence and presents an individual with the capacity to achieve enlightenment through the application of true will.

When Bob had read this the first time he had stopped at this point so I hadn't realized that the description continued:

Just as the six pointed star presents the quintessence or soul emanating from the combination of the four physical elements, the cross produced by the combination of the four worlds of existence intersects at the fountainhead of creation; the crown from which all life springs.

Because it was so cryptic, I had to read the passage through a couple of times before it sunk in.

The Universe represented God.

I had a revelation then.

In my mind's eye I saw the gypsy holding in her hand the three two pound coins. She tossed one into the air and it transformed into the cross symbol from my t-shirt and then the Universe Tarot card. I focussed on the centre of the cross, where all life supposedly manifests and my mind went back to the words I had read about the Magician: *'...the second member of the holy trinity, the Son.'*

My God, it's the holy trinity, I thought, *these cards represent the holy trinity!*

I looked back at the Universe image again. God – *The Father.* Then I rifled quickly back to the Magician – *The Son.* Finally, I turned to the page about the Strength card and scanned its description. My heart felt like it had stopped as I slowly read the words: *the Strength card can be linked to the Christian Trinity as it represents the third member, the Holy Ghost.*

Trembling and cold, the world around me seemed to be moving in slow motion; everything felt unreal and insubstantial, like a reflection on a lake easily disrupted by the slightest ripple.

My mind presented an image of my alarm clock with those all too familiar digits glaring back at me in luminous red.

I had asked for a sign. And got one quite literally from my alarm clock.

I laughed, slightly hysterically.

Sign of the time. I thought.

- The Fool –

A week later and my face was starting to look marginally better – I was out of the hospital, but didn't have to go back to work yet. Fortunately I had a good excuse not to go out robbing with Terry too – I said that my face would be too memorable – people were much more likely to remember someone coming into the shop with two black eyes every day and might start attributing the stolen books to me. Terry couldn't argue with this logic, for once, and as a result, with no-one watching his back, he didn't risk it. But this meant that he couldn't afford alcohol every day. So, he ended up spending a lot more time with Bob and smoking *his* weed instead, and, with Bob's supplies running low, the idea of doing the deal with Spider started to look more and more attractive. And of course, Terry was right there like a devil on Bob's shoulder.

'Spider's not going to wait around forever, Bob. Strike while the iron's hot mate! I saw him yesterday, you know.'

'Yeah? What did he say?

'He wondered what the fuck you were playing at and said that he had a few other parties who were interested in taking advantage of the deal of the century.'

Bob toked on his bong. We were back in his shoebox bedroom, eyes stinging with the orange zest air freshener.

'I still think it's a bad idea, Bob' I said.

Terry shot me one of his evil looks. 'Shut up Panda face!'

'Oh, that's tight, man.' Said Bob, laughing.

'Look, there's one thing I didn't tell you about the night I was sick round Flints...'

'Lighty whitey, ha ha!' Terry said, putting on a voice that resembled his junky housemate, Jed.

'No, listen this is important. I've been having lots of pretty mind blowing experiences on pot recently and...'

'Oh great, here we go, another one of Hemsy's fantastic tales coming up. Come on then Jackanory, tell us a story.' Said Terry.

Bob laughed again. Because they had been spending more time together, Terry had managed to ingratiate himself a lot more with Bob - of course he had, he had transformed himself from an embarrassing alcoholic into a smoking buddy. And what was I? I was just a lightweight who tried my damndest to *not* smoke pot, lest I go completely insane.

'Alright, well, you know how Flint's stash went missing that night, yeah? And this is a stash that was apparently supplied by Spider's contacts up north, from a hydroponic farm that he had to close down...'

'Yeah, yeah, we know all this, Hems – get to the point!' demanded Terry.

'Alright, well, you know how all of the dealers in Weymouth seem to be dry at the moment, including Fudge?'

Bob nodded and Terry just sat there with a look of indignation, not wanting Bob to be dissuaded from doing the deal.

'Well,' I continued, 'when I was there that night I heard a couple of blokes talking and they said that Fudge did the same deal with Spider that Flint did, and Fudge's stash also mysteriously went missing. They reckoned that Spider was just going from dealer to dealer, cleaning them out of cash by selling them a deal they couldn't refuse but then stealing it back the minute their back was turned...'

'Do you really think that Spider would be that dumb, Hems?' Terry said in a deep voice.

'Why not? He would effectively have a complete monopoly on the quite lucrative drug scene down here as well as cleaning out all of the drug dealers of their hard earned dough – making it impossible, or at least very hard, to get their hands on more.'

'Alright, Hems, if that's true, why would he also target, Bob, who's not a dealer, eh?'

'Easy target.' I replied. It was a mistake.

'Fuck off Hems', Bob said, using Terry's address, 'do I look like a fucking easy target, or are you saying that I'm thick?'

'I didn't mean that...' I began.

Terry didn't waste a moment to pour fuel on the fire.

'Oooh! Ooooh! He's calling you a fucking chump, Bob.'

'What? Don't be stupid!' I said.

'So now you're calling *me* stupid, Hems? Do you want me to put your nose back on the *other* side of your face for you - might be an improvement.'

'This is ridiculous', I said. I looked at Bob and he was still fuming, his blue eyes stony and his face flushed with red. I couldn't believe how easily Terry had manipulated him. Maybe it was something to do with the copious amounts of pot they smoked. Certainly it made *me* paranoid.

'Alright, Mark,' Bob said calmly, appearing to stifle his rage. 'Who exactly was it who said this about Fudge being cleaned out? Because when we left, there was only Spider, Goodman and a couple of girls there, and you said that Flint never came back till later, and if *he* said it then he would clearly have targeted Spider as the bloke who stole his stash, which would mean that Spider would be swimming with the fishes right now, not walking the streets bold as brass.'

I hesitated.

'Come on, Hems, who was it? Or are you just making it up?' Taunted Terry, giving me a poke to the ribs.

'Ow, you fucking prick!' I shouted.

Bob suddenly got up and pushed me backwards on the bed so that my head gonged off the radiator that I was lying against. His face had turned the colour of beetroot now and he was pointing in my face, very close to my still painful broken nose.

'Keep your fucking voice down, Hems! My gran's upstairs for fuck's sake – you could scare her!'

I put my hands up. Trying to understand how I ended up in this position. I looked around at Terry who gave me the sort of mischievous grin that a child might present after getting a sibling into trouble. In a minute he would probably start sticking his tongue out at me behind Bob's back.

'Anyway, Hems,' Terry said, his voice low, making sure he did not aggravate Bob, who was still very wound up and likely to explode at the slightest thing. 'You still haven't told us who said this about Spider supposedly doing the dirty on Fudge.'

It was as if he knew.

'Yeah, come on, Hems – tell us, because I swear if you made this whole thing up...'

'Alright, look I'm not making it up, I honestly heard this, but...'

I thought that if I lied at this point, they would recognize it and I'd be in trouble, so I decided to tell the truth.

'I heard it on TV.'

'What?' said Bob, incredulously.

'Well, I know it sounds absolutely fucking crazy, but I think pot makes me a bit psychic or clairvoyant or something and I can see things and tap into things sometimes. Anyway, *Eastenders* was on TV and I genuinely *heard* the characters saying all this stuff about Spider.'

Bob and Terry just stared at me, then Terry began to laugh.

'Are you fucking serious? He is, he's fucking serious Bob!'

Bob's anger seeped out of him in an instant and he started to laugh as well.

I couldn't help myself, it was infectious, so I started to laugh too.

'Honestly', I said doing my best to stifle the laughter, 'it was Phil and Grant...'

This gave them proper belly laughs and Bob, trying desperately to stop laughing, picked up a cushion and playfully threw it into my face.

Finally stifling the laughter, Bob said, 'Oh you're something else, Hemsy, you really are. I was here genuinely starting to believe you, but all along I've had nothing to worry about! Fuck it, let's do this.'

Terry clapped his hands loudly and whooped as Bob picked up his mobile.

'Terry, have you got Jed's number?'

'Yeah, why?'

'I ain't chancing this going Pete Tong mate, I want to make sure that we've got some backup if the shit hits the fan - and Jed's got a gun.'

'Yeah but it's only an air rifle.'

'Yeah, well hopefully that should suffice.'

'Fucking hell Bob, you're gangsta man!'

'Just shut up and give me his number.' demanded Bob, his serious face on.

'Ok, ok', said Terry scrolling through his contacts and finding Jed's number. He said the digits aloud and Bob typed them into his phone. After a few moments I heard a crackly voice at the end of the line.

'Hello? Jed? Listen mate, it's Bob, no Terry's mate Bob. Yeah, not bad thanks, listen man I was wondering if you would be interested in doing a little bit of business for me. No, not that sort of business, something that will utilize the training you received in your previous occupation. No, not making pizzas, the other occupation - you know when you were a paratrooper. Yeah, look I don't want to say too much, but if you could do this favour for me there would be a really nice juicy payment for you, you know what I mean. Well, I don't want to discuss it over the phone but I'll tell you all about it in person. Great! Ok mate, do you know where wheeley hill is on Portland? Yeah that's the one, at the back of Easton. Can you come and meet me there at seven? Nice one, Jed. I'll see you soon. Oh and Jed, almost forgot, you know that thing you use to get rid of the birds in the morning? Can you bring that along too – discreetly of course. Brilliant – cheers man. I'll see you at seven. Bye.'

'Fucking hell, Bob. Do you really think that Spider is going to try and nick the weed back? Come on, Hemsy's just mental.'

'Like I say, just a precaution. Anyway guys, be quiet a minute yeah.' Bob found another number on his mobile phone and pressed the call button.

There was a long pause where I hoped that Spider would not pick up but then, to my dismay, I heard a voice at the other end of the line.

'Hello Spider, it's Bob – how's it going mate?'

This time I moved a little closer to Bob so I could just make out the voice at the other end of the line.

'Mr Bainbury, now *there's* a turn-up for the books,' said Spider, his voice laced with good humour and something else I couldn't quite put my finger on – relish?

'Thought you'd wussed out, knew you wouldn't though, Bob, always knew you had half a brain.'

Personally, I would take this as an insult, but Bob seemed to take it as a compliment.

'I'd like to take advantage of the little business opportunity we discussed.' Said Bob.

'I've no doubt, Mr Bainbury and I'm glad to hear it, however, the game has changed – there's another player involved and they've brought an extra monkey to the party, know what I mean?'

Bob seemed a little puzzled.

'The price of the game, Bob, has gone up by five hundred.'

Bob considered this for a moment.

'Alright – should be able to stretch to that.'

'Excellent news, Mr Bainbury. Where would you like to meet?'

'You know that place we did business last time, on Portland?'

'Indeed I do - good choice. What time?'

'Can you make it for seven thirty tonight?'

'Oooh, I'll see what I can do but might be pushing it more towards eight now I'm afraid.'

'Ok, eight o'clock will be fine. See you then.' Bob said, pressing the end button on the phone.

'Fuck.' I said.

'Shut up, Hems,' said Bob. 'Boys, can you do me a favour and just step outside a minute so I can get under the bed please?'

'Sure.' We said in unison, standing up. Terry slid the door open and barged his way past me, always wanting to be first.

When we were out the door, Bob had enough room to open a slide door on the side of his bed. He had loosened the thin wood of the base so that it could be lifted to reveal the floorboards underneath. Lifting one of these, he retrieved a large shoebox and placed it on the bed. Still on his knees, he opened the shoebox to reveal several large wads of cash.

'Jesus!' said Terry, 'you're minted mate.'

'Shhhhh Terry!' said Bob turning round with a grimace, 'I don't want my Mom to find out, so come back in here and close the door.'

We did as he said and watched as he counted the money.

'I don't believe it, I'm thirty quid shy. Can you boys help me out?'

'Well I don't even think you should do this, Bob.' I said.

'Oh, come on Hemsy, I have to do this now! You know that! Now are you my mate or what?'

I looked at him, his face pleading and drew out my wallet.

'I only have a twenty. Hold on, I'll see if I have any more.'

I went into my pockets and drew out two pounds, twenty two pence. Hah! I laughed – maybe Bob was meant to do this deal all along?

'What's up, Hems?' said Bob.

'Nothing, I only have two pound twenty two more though.'

'Ok, Terry?'

'Ok, Bob I have a tenner but this is all I've got to get food for the rest of the week, alright.'

'Don't worry boys – you will be well recompensed, have no doubt about that!' Bob said, taking the twenty off me and the ten off Bob and leaving me with my change.

He added the notes to his wads and recounted just to make sure. Terry watched, rubbing his hands and smiling, clearly relishing the action.

'Eight grand.' He said, finishing his count, the money now neatly separated into eight large wads, bound with elastic bands. He placed the money back into the box and then retrieved a black backpack from beneath his bed and placed the shoebox inside this. He looked at his watch and said: 'Six thirty, shit, we'd better start making a move to go and meet old matey boy.'

'Let's *do* this.' Said Terry.

- The Blasted Tower -

Twenty minutes later and we were parking up in a dark and secluded lane at the foot of *Wheeley* hill. I'm pretty sure that's not its actual name and probably just something Bob made up as a kid because it was where he used to go and practice wheelies on his BMX. I vaguely remembered him telling me how he had gone too fast down the hill one day and had come a cropper, flying over the handlebars and losing two of his teeth in the process. It was a fairly steep hill with a pit at the bottom, and you couldn't really see what was going on in the pit unless you were in it or up the hill. This, combined with the fact that we were already on a quiet island and about twenty minutes away from the nearest house, made this the perfect place for a drug deal. Especially if you had someone providing cover from the hillside just in case things went *Pete Tong*, as Bob had put it.

Getting out of the car, we had a short walk to the foot of the hill. It was a crisp night and I could see my breath in front of me as we walked. It was very dark here, with not a street light in sight, but fortunately it was a clear night too so the moon and stars provided just enough light to prevent us from walking into one another.

Reaching the bottom of the hill, Bob frantically scanned the area.

'Where the fuck is he?'

'Don't sweat it, Bob, he'll be here.' Said Terry.

'Yeah well that's easy for you to say isn't it Terry, you're not the one standing there with,' he lowered his voice, 'eight fucking grand in your bag, are you?'

'Alright, just chill out, he'll be here.'

'He does know where this is doesn't he?'

'Yeah, he was with us that time we met Flint here, remember?'

'Oh, yeah.' Bob said, looking at his watch again.

'Oi oi lads!' Shouted a shadowy figure ambling towards us from halfway up the hill.

'Jed? Keep your voice down man!' Bob half whispered, half shouted.

'So-R-ry.' Jed said. 'What's with all the cloak and dagger eh? You boys planning a fuckin heist or somet?'

'Something like that.' Said Bob.

'Alright Jedbo, how you doing?'

'I told you not to call me that, Terry you little prick.'

'Ha ha – sorry, Jed.' Said Terry nervously.

'Will you girls shut up.' Said Bob, clearly anxious. This is serious, we don't have a lot of time.'

'Alright, Bainbury, what's the plan then Mr boss man? And, er, more importantly what do I get out of this?'

'First of all, tell me you brought your rifle with you.'

'Rifle? What are you talking about?'

'Oh shit! I told you to bring your fucking rifle man!'

'No you never.'

'Yes, I did, I told you to bring that thing you use to scare the birds in the morning.'

'Oh! I thought you were talking about my cock mate – I brought that.'

Bob turned around and looked at Terry incredulously. 'Is he fucking serious?'

'Course I'm not serious, you old woman, I'm just pulling your chain init. I've got the gun here.' He presented a long case and waggled it in front of Bob's nose, smiling.

'Jesus, Jed, don't do that to me man!'

'Ok, what's the deelio, chief?'

'Ok, come with me. You boys wait here,' he said, making his way up the hill. 'About halfway up this hill there's a little nook where I want you to hide. We won't be able to see you, but you should have a good view of this whole area. Here we are.' He indicated a small crater in the side of the hill.

'Better not be muddy,' said Jed.

'Don't worry it hasn't rained in a while so it should be ok.'

'Bloody cold though. If my bollocks freeze together down here, Bobby boy, I'll be expecting hearty compensation!'

'Yeah, right', said Bob, stepping back a few paces down the hill to assess whether Jed could be seen. He couldn't – he was completely immersed in shadow.

'Ok, that's good. Now, in about...' Bob looked at his watch, 'twenty minutes we are going to be meeting with some pretty serious characters. All I want you to do is watch and cover our backs, ok? It should just be a straight exchange and a handshake but if these guys give us any trouble, I want you to shoot 'em in the legs or something, ok?'

'Sounds like a sweet job to me matey – but what are you going to do for me.' He took the rifle out of the bag and pointed at Bob.

'Don't point that fucking thing at me, Jed!' Bob said, grabbing the end of the rifle and shoving it to the side.

'Alright, alright, I'm just fucking with you.' Jed said, lowering the weapon and kneeling down. 'Seriously though, what do I get for supplying this little, er, service?'

'I'll give you an ounce of the finest weed around.'

'An ounce? You're 'avin a fuckin giraffe mate!'

'Alright, I'll give you an ounce and a half.'

'Bollocks will you – if I have to shoot someone, that could be fuckin jail time man, I ain't risking *that* for a poxy ounce and alf.' He started making his way back to his feet.

'Alright, two ounces, final offer.'

'Three - and that's *my* final offer.'

Bob considered this. This was a tiny fraction of the amount he was going to get but obviously Jed didn't know this.

'Alright Jed, you win – three ounces.'

'Yeah? Fuckin A!'

'But only if you do a fucking first class job up here.'

'For three ounces, Bob, I'll shine your nob as well if you like.'

'That won't be necessary, thanks.' He started making his way back down the hill and then looked around. From this high up he could see his car parked up in the narrow lane. 'I just thought, can you give us a signal when you see anyone approaching?'

'What sort of signal?'

'I don't know, like an owl call or something.'

'Erm, Okeykokey.'

'Alright, now stay low and when you see us leave, just stay put for a bit until everyone's gone and then give me a call and we'll meet up later.'

Jed replied with a salute and Bob made his way back down the hill.

Having given Jed his orders, Bob was now pacing back and forth at the bottom of the hill, looking at his watch every ten seconds.

I could see that Terry wanted to tell Bob to chill out again but thought better of it. Instead, he turned to me.

'So Hems, did you manage to remember who gave you that beating on the beach yet?'

'No.' I said, 'it's doing my head in actually, it's horrible not knowing what the bastards looked like. I keep thinking that I could bump into them at any time and not know it – I mean, just yesterday I passed a group of blokes on the street and started to get paranoid thinking to myself – it could have been you! Was it you?'

'Yeah that's pretty fucked up, I tell you thou...'

<Two-oo-two-oo-two-oo>

I saw the red digits of my alarm clock superimposed on the night. 'What was that?' I said, more than a little freaked out.

<Two-oo-two-oo-two-oo>

'It's Jed's signal – they're here boys. Right, just act cool and let me do the talking.'

I straightened. What if I was wrong about that sign, what if it was a warning? What if it meant, *get the fuck out of there, Mark?* More paranoia, I could hardly run away now, could I?

Three figures approached us from the left. I could make out the relatively slender figure of Spider almost immediately, partly because he was significantly shorter than the other two, who each must have been about six foot four and partly because of the lithe way in which he walked – like a cat.

‘Good evening, gentlemen.’ Said Spider with a wolfish grin. ‘Mr Bainbury’, Bob nodded, ‘Terry.’

‘Alright Spider,’ said Terry.

‘And who’s that in the shadows? Oh, hello, Mr Hems, how are we all doing this evening?’

‘Alright mate.’ I said and ‘not bad.’

‘These are my associates, Mr Pink and Mr White.’

We all stared at the large men, their faces could have been carved out of stone.

‘Ha ha!’ Spider exclaimed, ‘I’m just fucking with ya, these are me mates Ron and Charlie. We go way back. Anyway, let's get down to business shall we. Do you have the readies, Mr Bainbury?’

‘Eight grand.’ Said Bob. Taking the backpack from his back.

‘Lovely.’ Said Spider putting his hand out to accept the bag.

‘Hold on there, Spider, let’s see the merch first, yeah?’

Spider's smile dropped. 'Of course .'

The man on Spiders left came forward revealing a large black carryall, which he dropped at Bob's feet.

Before relinquishing his cash, Bob crouched and unzipped the carryall to reveal countless plastic bags filled with what appeared to be skunk. He withdrew one of the bags and opened it, removing one of the buds for inspection. Of course, it was pitch black so he struggled to see the detail in the dark.

'Here let me help you with that', said Spider, 'Charlie, can you shed a little light on proceedings please?'

The man on Spider's right came forward and produced a pen light which he shone onto Bob's hands, causing us all to squint against the sudden glare. Bob examined the weed again and crystals shone on his fingers. Appearing to be satisfied, he gave the bag a good sniff and then said: 'Nice.'

'Happy?' said Spider.

'Happy. Though obviously I'm going to have to trust you that it's all here as I don't have any scales with me and this might take a while to weigh.'

'Bob, Bob – how long have you known me, eh? I'm not gonna go and do the dirty on me mates now, am I?'

<Two-oo-two-oo-two-oo>

We all jumped.

'What was that?' said Spider, his men scanning the hillside.

'Dunno', said Bob, 'sounded like an owl to me.'

'An owl?' said Spider, 'Oh', he paused, looking around. 'But there are no trees around here..?'

'Something's a bit fishy ere, Spider, think we'd better move.' Said goon number one, Charlie.

'Yeah, think you're right.' Said Spider suspicion rising on his face. 'Hand over the ready's please, Mr Bainbury.'

'Sure.' Said Bob, passing over the bag.

Spider got to one knee and quickly unzipped the bag and pulled out the large cardboard box.

'Light please, Charlie.' He said and Charlie directed the beam at the now open box.

He pulled out a note from the middle of one of the stacks and examined it under the light before proceeding to roughly assess the amount in each bundle.

'Come on, Spider, let's move.' Said goon number two, Ron. 'I don't like this'.

'Ok, Ok.' Said Spider, 'Bob, I'm going to have to trust *you* on this too, but I'm sure you're a man of your word.'

Before Bob could answer, a figure emerged from the darkness to our left and something glinted in the moonlight at Bob's neck.

'What the fuck?' said Bob, trying to wrestle a hand away from his throat.

'Now, now, Bob, I wouldn't do that if I were you, this is a pretty sharp knife.' It was Flint, he must have tailed Spider right to us.

Out of nowhere I felt a hard jab to the face and fell to the floor as pain exploded in my recently broken nose and my world went red.

'That's for getting off with my missus.' Said Goodman emerging from the shadows. As I attempted to get up, he grabbed me by the hair and spat in my face.

'Whoa, whoa, what's going on, Flint?' Demanded Spider.

'What's going on? Well let's just say I've been doing some digging into the little matter of my five kilos going missing and do you know what I found out?'

'You had it up your arse all along?' Queried Spider, 'you're certainly full of something, Flint.'

'Ha ha, always the wise-arse aren't you Spider.' Retorted Flint, 'Hmmm, *Spider* - that's a good name for you really isn't it, 'cos that's what you're like - enticing all us flies into your fucking web and then robbing us blind!' He pushed the knife further into Bob's throat and a drop of blood appeared.

'Alright, now, Flint, just calm down yeah?'

'Calm down? Fuck you, Spider! Let me tell you what I found out 'cos I'm sure these boys will be interested in this little story as well. Turns out you see, that our friendly neighbourhood Spidey here has been going around *all* the dealers in Weymouth and pulling the same trick. He'll sell you the *deal of the century* and then *nick* off with your weed - leaving you out of *fucking* dope and out of cash.'

Suddenly Terry ran at Goodman, punching him hard in the side of the face and causing him to lose his grip on me.

Flint looked around and lowered the knife slightly. This was all the chance Bob needed. He bit hard into Flint's wrist.

Flint yelled out in pain, dropping the knife to the ground. Bob immediately elbowed him in the stomach and he went down on one knee.

'That's the second and last time you put a knife to me, you cunt!' said Bob, kicking Flint in the face. Flint toppled backwards against the side of the hill, his face gushing blood.

While this was going on, Terry was wrestling on the floor with Goodman.

Bob picked up the black carryall and got to his feet.

'Come on, Mark, Terry! Let's get out of here.'

'I'll be right behind you!' said Terry, still struggling with Goodman.

'Sorry, Bob, I can't let you do that,' said Spider, his goons stepping in front of us to block our path.

'Hand over the bag please.'

Bob looked genuinely betrayed and when he looked up at Spider, his eyes were cold.

'Jeeed!' he yelled.

A puzzled look appeared on Spider's face and he looked around at the hillside. Looking back at Bob he was about to say something when the pellet hit him in the neck and he went flying into the goon named Charlie.

'Wha?' Began Charlie as a pellet hit him in the arm, his other arm socking Spider in the head as he corkscrewed around to assess the damage. Spider sprawled into the hillside, apparently out for the count. But the bullets kept flying and Charlie yelled out in pain as he disappeared into the pit.

Witnessing this, Ron looked up at the hill and started to make his way in the direction of Jed's hideout. He didn't get very far before he too yelled out in pain, clutching his face and falling to his knees.

'Fuck! Come on, Mark.' Shouted Bob starting to run.

'Terry!' I shouted, looking around. He had Goodman in a headlock on the floor.

'I'm alright, Mark. Go! I'll be right behind you! Run!'

Adrenaline coursing through my body, I cast one last look at Terry and then ran after Bob.

I reached the car just in time to see the headlights obliterate the darkness in front of Bob's car. He had been blocked in by Spider's black Saab and was smacking the steering wheel in frustration – a look of defeat on his face. I stopped dead, feeling defeated myself. If we tried to get out of there on foot we were unlikely to make it in time, they would probably catch up to us and mow us down.

A guttural scream echoed around the hills in the near distance 'Baiiiiiiiinbury!' It was Flint. He was probably already after us. That launched me into action and I ran at the Saab and started to push with all my strength.

'Hemsy, what are you doing, that's not gonna wor...' He stopped mid sentence because he could see that it *was* working. As I pushed, the car slowly began to slide into the ditch at the side of the road.

Giving one last almighty push, the car rolled down the side of the bank and disappeared into the darkness.

Amazed and suddenly completely drained, I looked down at my arms in the yellow glare of the headlights.

'Baiiiiinbury!' Flint roared, now much closer.

'Quick Mark, get in.' Yelled Bob.

I ran around the car and yanked the door open. Diving inside, Bob had his foot on the accelerator before I closed the door.

But we weren't out of the woods yet. There was a loud smash as the rear window exploded, tiny fragments of glass showering the passenger seat.

I looked back to see Flint, blood failing to mask the scowl on his face. He must have thrown a brick at the window and was now sprinting towards us – a demon painted red by the glow of the rear lights. Bob hammered the accelerator and Flint was enveloped by the darkness.

'Fucking hell!' I said, looking at Bob. He was shaking but his eyes remained glued on the road as we sped forward. Sweat trickling down his face.

'Where are we going?' I asked.

Bob didn't seem to hear me.

'Bob?'

'Dunno, Hems. Away. Just gotta get the fuck out of here.'

'Do you think Terry's ok?'

'I hope so', he paused, checking his rear view mirror, 'I think they'll be more concerned about getting out of there with the cash to be honest.'

'Yeah, but they could use Terry as a hostage or something.'

'Well hopefully Jed will have taken care of them so that Terry could get away. Hope he had enough pellets in that gun.'

'Yeah. Jesus it's a good job he was there otherwise we'd have been *fucked* man.'

'Yep, best money I ever spent. Damn, should have taken the shortcut! Fuck!'

He looked in the rear view mirror again. 'How did you do that Mark?'

'What?'

'What do you mean, *what*? You just pushed over a *car* man!'

I shrugged, 'Well you know me, Bob, strong as a lion.' I said, still shaking.

Bob gave me a puzzled look and then returned his eyes to the road, just in time to see headlights rapidly approaching from the left.

There was a sudden impact and I was thrown violently to the side as the car jack-knifed to the left, absorbing the impact of the crash before screeching to a halt halfway up the curb.

I felt tiny fragments of glass under my fingers and could smell the acrid odour of petrol and burnt rubber. I slowly sat up, wincing at a pain in my arm and saw that it had been badly grazed. It hurt to move my neck but I looked up to check if Bob was okay. He must have hit his head against the stereo because *Live Forever* by Oasis began to blare from the speakers.

'You alright Hems?' he said, a trickle of blood running down the side of his head.

'Think so', I said, 'you?'

'Yeah'

Dazed and winded, I brought my hand to my neck, where I had no doubt sustained a bit of nasty whiplash, and looked out of the rear window at the other car. I shielded my eyes against the glare of one of the headlights – the other must have been smashed in the collision - and I could just make out the shadowy form of the driver behind a vale of smoke. It was Flint. He was once again bathed in red light and as I watched he raised his head and smiled a terrible smile, his face now covered in blood. Looking directly at me with those piercing dark eyes, his knife glinted in the moonlight as he performed a throat slitting gesture.

'Bob? We gotta move!' I shouted.

Bob looked dazed and confused and I hoped he hadn't sustained a head injury in the collision.

As I watched in horror, Flint began to emerge from the car.

'Bob!' I said, shaking his shoulder.

'What?' asked Bob, vacantly.

'We've gotta go, Flint's...'

There was a loud smash, a shower of glass and a flurry of movement as strong arms grabbed hold of my t shirt and began to yank me upwards.

I struggled to break free and then heard the roar of the engine as the car sped forwards and Flint was forced to let go of me.

The cold air raged through the broken windows and the smell of burnt rubber and petrol sharpened my already taught senses. I looked back and saw that Flint was making his way back into his car to pursue us.

'Fucking hell!' I shouted, 'what is this guy, the fucking *Terminator* or something!'

Bob looked into his rear view mirror.

'Well he's certainly not giving up.'

As we approached the top of the road that had often plagued my nightmares, I became aware of a loud clanging coming from the left wheel and we began to lose speed.

'What is it?'

'It's fucked that's what it is.'

'Oh no', I said, 'not now!

'Baiiiiiiinbury!' Flint roared as his car wrestled past us on the right hand side. He was laughing maniacally as he swerved into the side of Bob's car. We veered dangerously to the left giving me a terrifying view over the side of the cliff: An abyss of black, the sea twinkling in the moonlight three hundred feet below. I had a sudden vision of the *Blasted Tower* Tarot card - the one with the two men falling to their deaths, and started to make out the features of the second person. It was like the tapeworm dream all over again.

There was another loud crunch as Flint's car smashed into the side of us and Bob wrestled with the steering wheel, only just keeping us on the road.

I gasped with relief, but it was short lived. As I looked towards the other car I was just in time to see Flint ramming his steering wheel to the left once again.

There was another loud smash and the tyres screeched as I was forced against the window, the night air cold at my side. And then the cars began to spin as they became locked in a perilous pirouette.

Everything slowed down then, as the cars spun. I took in every detail, Flint's smile receding to reveal the face of a frightened child; Bob, struggling to right the car's doomed trajectory as it hurtled towards the edge of the cliff - the two men wearing the same expression of panic and fear as the recognition of their mutual fates gripped them.

And then we were in the cold air, weightless for a moment as the gaping night rushed up to devour us.

Into the darkness I fell as my soul was stripped apart.

I was being *erased.* Piece by piece, memory by memory, thought by thought - the very fabric of my being unravelling into the night like the threads of an elaborate tapestry. I struggled to hold on to life, wrestling with unconsciousness as the cold wind ravaged my mind.

But it was not yet the end.

Just as I thought I was doomed to live out eternity in darkness, lightning lit up the void with a *bang* and I hurtled towards its source. I tried to shield my eyes against the glare but realized I couldn't. My hands didn't seem to be there anymore – my *body* didn't seem to be there anymore! Terrified, I was helpless as I fell into the lightning. And witnessed my own birth: Screaming, I emerged from my mother's womb, dripping with blood and warmth and life.

The world was radiant with colour and verve and the sound of my own crying threatened to deafen me – but I was alive! There was an odd feeling of weightlessness as I was carried through the air and then my mother's face came into view: tears streaming down red cheeks as she took me into her arms. She hugged me close and my heart leapt with the sheer wonder of the moment. I wanted to talk to her - to explain what had happened, but as I opened my mouth to speak the lightning sounded with a bang and I was ripped forwards in time.

I found myself padding on almost new feet to a young man I barely recognized as my father before the lightning ripped me away again.

Bang!

I saw my first day at school, spraying macaroni with gold paint.

Bang!

My big sister placing a plaster on my knee.

Bang!

Tiny happy faces crammed with cake and joy at a forgotten birthday party.

Bang!

My long dead dog, Benjy.

Bang!

My first kiss – a flurry of pig-tales and red ribbons.

Bang!

My brother being born, his little red face crusty with snot.

Bang! Bang! Bang!

The memories came faster and faster - all of the people I had known, all of my triumphs, all of my failures. Until I sensed with terror that the final event was approaching. With a churning dread I heard the screeching of tyres, felt the cold wind in my face and saw the anguished faces of a friend and an enemy spinning around me before a relentless ocean rushed up to envelop us.

And then nothing.

I was once again plummeting through the darkness. I tried to remember how I got there but with growing dismay I realized that my memories had been eaten up by the darkness, discarded in time. But still I fell, nothing more than a collection of thoughts now - only just able to recognize that the farther I fell, the less I became. *Soon I will be nothing,* I thought, and with this notion, a barely conscious fragment of self questioned the nature of its state and had an epiphany: if there were a *correlation* between my descent and my demise, then what if I could somehow reverse the trend, if I could fight gravity's pull and *ascend*? What if death was simply a type of downward current, reflected by my descent? Could I reverse the current? Could I somehow climb back to life? And what if I pushed farther, beyond even the ceiling of life, perhaps to its final conclusion? Where might that lead?

What if the single, most important purpose of all life was to evolve will to the extent that it might defy the mortal coil, break the physical bonds and hurtle skywards in an attempt to better itself. To better the Universe?

- Afterword -

You may be surprised to learn that most of the events in this book actually did transpire, with the exception of my death of course. The horrific crash at the end of the book was however based on an actual incident that occurred on Old road, Portland, Dorset, claiming the lives of two young men.

Even the gypsy was real, though I actually came across her while I was on holiday in Cornwall. I'm embarrassed to say that she actually took three twenty pound notes from me and *not* three two pound coins, so mesmerised was I by the personal details that she somehow knew about me.

At the heart of this book lies a quest for meaning and asks the question, *Is there a God*? I must stress that this book by no means attests to provide proof for the existence of God. However, the 222 phenomena *is* real and countless people report it on a daily basis on forums such as www.doyouseee222.com and www.222mystery.com, though recently both of these sites have mysteriously disappeared from the internet.

I was not able to acquire the rights to display the Tarot card images in this book at the time of publishing, but once again, the descriptions of those cards *are* real and they really do contain the symbols that were presented on the *Spirit of Harmony* t-shirt, also real.

If you are interested in taking a look at the Tarot cards described in this book they are part of a wonderful deck called *The Magickal Tarot,* produced by Antony Clark.

I believe that the connections between the numbers, the symbols, the tarot cards and the holy trinity may represent a true synchronicity.

Was it a sign from God? Well, maybe time will tell.

Mark Hems, Feb, 2013

Back of a U.S One Hundred Dollar Bill.

5110574R10155

Printed in Great Britain
by Amazon.co.uk, Ltd.,
Marston Gate.